*Max the stron...
with every intimate kiss.*

Max cupped Ariana with his hands, flicking his thumbs over her moistened flesh, while his kiss wandered across her collarbone and up her neck. Their lips clashed in a hot, breathless battle. She touched him everywhere. Down his back, up his arms, her fingers pushing through his hair, then dipping into his boxers. Learning him as he learned her.

He lifted her as he stood, letting her feet touch the ground long enough to remove the last scraps of clothing between them. Then he wrapped her legs around his waist and carried her to the ledge of the balcony.

Max settled her down and turned her toward the glorious view of the bridge and the bay drifting in and out of the fog. Twinkling lights appeared behind Ariana's heavy eyelids when Max slid his hand down her belly and through her dark curls, testing her need.

Stroking her gently, he said, "Open your eyes, Ari. I promised to show you the view."

Swallowing deeply, Ariana mumbled, "I don't need to see. I just want to feel."

Max tugged her earlobe with his teeth. "You can do both. Don't settle for less when you can have it all. When *we* can have it all."

Blaze™

Dear Reader,

This month marks the launch of a supersexy new series—
Harlequin Blaze. If you like love stories with a strong sexual
edge, then this is the line for you! The books are fun and
flirtatious, the heroes are hot and outrageous. Blaze is a
series for the woman who wants *more* in her reading
pleasure....

Leading off the launch is bestselling author
Vicki Lewis Thompson, who brings us a heroine to
remember in the aptly titled #1 *Notorious*. Then popular
Jo Leigh delivers a blazing story in #2 *Going for It*, about
a sex therapist who ought to take her own advice. One of
today's hottest writers, Stephanie Bond, spins a humorous
tale of sexual adventure in #3 *Two Sexy!* Rounding out
the month is talented Julie Elizabeth Leto with the romp
#4 *Exposed*, which exposes the sexy side of San Francisco
and is the first of the SEXY CITY NIGHTS miniseries.

Look for four Blaze books every month at your favorite
bookstore. And check us out online at eHarlequin.com
and tryblaze.com.

Enjoy!

Birgit Davis-Todd
Senior Editor & Editorial Coordinator
Harlequin Blaze

EXPOSED

Julie Elizabeth Leto

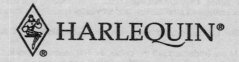

HARLEQUIN®

TORONTO • NEW YORK • LONDON
AMSTERDAM • PARIS • SYDNEY • HAMBURG
STOCKHOLM • ATHENS • TOKYO • MILAN • MADRID
PRAGUE • WARSAW • BUDAPEST • AUCKLAND

For the members of the Tampa Area Romance Authors (TARA), who continuously and generously buoy and cheer both my career and me. My success is rooted in your loving support.

ISBN 0-373-79008-2

EXPOSED

A NOTE FROM THE AUTHOR...

I vividly remember the day I fell in love with San Francisco. I was sixteen and on my first trip without my parents, visiting a place that was on the other side of the country. The romance, the craziness and the sensuality of the City by the Bay snared me instantly. It was a different world than anything I'd ever seen before—and I was in love!

Now I love to travel, and big cities are my favorite destinations. San Francisco. L.A. New York. When the idea behind the SEXY CITY NIGHTS miniseries came to me, I was in Chicago. The idea hit so hard, I nearly called my editor from my cell phone (which, to Toronto, isn't cheap!). The skyscrapers, the crowds, the nightlife—cities like San Francisco offer everything to everyone, if you're only willing to take a chance.

I hope you get as caught up in the SEXY CITY NIGHTS as I was that first time in San Francisco. Please drop me a line and let me know. You can write to me at P.O. Box 270885, Tampa, FL 33688-0885. Or, if you'd like to get a sneak peek at the next books in the series, link to my web site at www.Julieleto.com—and send me an e-mail while you're there!

Julie Elizabeth Leto

1

"Hey, sweet thing. Wanna lift?"

Ariana Karas swung her pack securely over her shoulder, ducking her head so the tube of architectural plans shoved inside didn't knock off her lucky hat. She secured the Greek fisherman's cap by pressing the brim firmly over her dark bangs and stepped onto the Powell-Hyde cable car for her ride back to the restaurant. She flashed a weary grin at Benny, the sixty-something brakeman who flirted with her on a nightly basis, just enough to make her smile—even tonight.

"Sweet thing?" she asked, eyebrow cocked. "I should be offended, Benny." She produced her transit slip.

Benny rubbed his bearded jowls and laughed. He released the lever and tweaked the bell, setting the car—empty except for her in the front and a group of chilled tourists riding inside—in motion up Powell Street toward Fisherman's Wharf.

"Heaven help me if I ever offend you, Miss Karas. That tube you've been carting from the restaurant to Market Street for the past few months would end up whacked upside my head."

Ariana laughed silently, wondering how Benny and everyone else in the world could ever get the idea that she was so tough. Sure, she talked a good game to keep her rowdy bar patrons in line or to ward off the aggressive transients that sometimes hung around in front of the restaurant, but on nights like tonight, Ariana relived all the uncertainty she'd felt when she'd left home, young and starved for independence. Against the wishes of her entire family—grandparents, father, mother, two brothers and two sisters— she'd packed up and moved across the country from Tarpon Springs, Florida, to San Francisco, California. She'd had a degree in accounting from the local junior college and little knowledge of the world outside her tight-knit Greek community.

But she'd also had dreams taller and wider than the Golden Gate Bridge. She'd wanted to be her own woman, make her own dreams come true—on her terms and with few debts owed to anyone when her lifetime of fantasies became reality.

Eight years had passed. And tonight, three years of marriage, one divorce and five years of fourteen-hour days later, she was one week away from seeing her dream begin. Starting tomorrow afternoon, the restaurant she operated would be closed for business for the first time since her uncle had turned management duties over to her. When the remodeling was done and she reopened, she'd have a large, airy, modern space to serve locals and tourists alike. Customers would line up to taste her eclectic blend of hearty Greek and Italian foods and sip original libations in her signature bar.

She'd call it *Ari's Oasis*.

She'd worked so long, so hard to compete with the other operations on the Wharf, some of which had been serving food to San Francisco since the turn of the century. Her uncle inherited the building from her aunt Sonia's family, fishermen who used to sell their catch from makeshift carts. The permanent structure had evolved over the years, but the crisp, white-paneled walls, quaint fishing nets strung from the ceiling and red checkerboard tablecloths, while homey, were showing their age. Even Uncle Stefano knew the time for change had come. But he enjoyed sipping strong Turkish coffee in the mornings and ouzo in the evenings with customers more than supervising the menu or balancing the books.

Ariana had left home specifically to work for Stefano and Sonia, in hopes of inheriting the business from her childless relatives. Marriage to Rick got in the way. But soon after Ariana found herself divorced and jobless, she'd accepted Stefano's offer to take over. In record time, she'd put the restaurant in the black and on the map, and had secured financing for much-needed renovations. She'd even approved every blue pencil mark on the prints she carried in her pack.

Now she had seven days—the contractors wouldn't arrive until a week from Monday—to clear out the place before they started knocking down walls. Since Uncle Stefano insisted that he supervise the moving of the equipment and furniture into storage, he ordered Ariana to take the week off—her first real vacation since she moved to California—to rejuvenate before her life descended into complete turmoil.

And who was she to argue? Stefano had a way of making his rare commands sound like sweet talk—a skill he'd developed to deal with his loving but willful wife. A woman Ari reminded him of, judging by the times he called her Sonia, particularly during a disagreement. Ari swallowed a bittersweet smile.

Sonia's death and Ari's divorce had been strong

catalysts to her single-minded pursuit of success for the restaurant. She'd worked tirelessly for five years. But now she really needed a break. For herself. For her sanity.

The cable car rattled and shook as it moved uphill, a familiar buzzing hum beneath her feet and a crisp San Francisco night chilling her cheeks. The fog was rolling in late tonight. Fingers of smoky moisture twirled toward them from the Bay. But over her shoulder the scene was clear—the glittering neon and historic charm that was San Francisco.

The cable car paused between the intersections at Geary and Powell, then shrugged forward when no one jumped aboard at Union Square. The main cable car traffic at this time of night was on the return trip, from the Wharf to the hotels at Market Street and stops along the way. At least, that's what she'd heard.

On most Friday nights, and Saturday through Thursday as well, she was helping her hostess find seats for customers, checking on orders with her chef or serving her specialty drinks in the bar. She knew little to nothing about the charming, diverse, any-thing-goes city she called home. Her explorations were limited to the nightspots her former husband once played with his band and the blocks around Chi-natown where she lived in a rent-controlled apartment above Madame Li's Herb Shop.

But she had one week to see the city, every inch of it if she could, before she immersed herself in su-pervising the contractors who would turn her quaint dockside eatery into a restaurant of international rep-utation.

Before she could contemplate what her father would think of her bold, risky move from storefront eatery to full-fledged culinary powerhouse, a flutter of glossy pages caught her eye from farther down the bench, snared by a groove in the wood. She slid over and plucked the magazine from the seat, recognizing it as one of the hip women's periodicals her landlady bought for her shop so the older patrons who stopped by for her delicious blend of tea and gossip could laugh at their younger counterparts and their silly ideas of womanhood.

She might have agreed with them about some of the magazine's topics, but this issue's feature caught Ari's eye.

Sexy City Nights: San Francisco Style.

Sex. Now *there* was an interesting activity Ari barely remembered. She fanned the pages until she found the large color spread featuring a couple leaning against the bright orange railing of the Golden Gate. Darkness and a fine mist of fog shadowed the models' bodies, but their faces were angled into the photographer's light just enough to capture expressions. Wanton desire on the man's. Sheer ecstasy in the eyes of the woman.

Whatever he was doing to her, she was enjoying it.

A lot.

The cable car rattled along, slowing beneath a bright street lamp long enough for Ariana to see that the man's left hand had disappeared somewhere beneath the woman's incredibly short and fluttering skirt.

Ari swallowed, briefly marveling at the bold sensuality of this mainstream magazine. But soon her intimacy-starved imagination superimposed her own face, equally enraptured, equally pleasured, over the model in the photograph. A pressure, not unlike the sensation of a man's fingers, slipped between her thighs and stirred a throbbing loneliness she usually felt only late at night after a hot shower or early in the morning after a restless battle with erotic dreams.

How thrilling, how inviting—to be in a public place while a man touched you privately—with only the night and the thin misty remnants of fog to shield the sensations from prying eyes. For a woman to risk such discovery, the desire for a man's touch and utter need for intimacy would have to override every ounce of good sense, every inkling of decent behavior.

Ari sighed. Once upon a time, she'd been caught up in a man enough to leave her logic at the door. Unfortunately, though the sex hadn't been bad, her ex-husband, Rick, had been more concerned with his own pleasure than hers. And she, barely into her twenties and wholly inexperienced, hadn't known better.

On the bumpy road to now, she'd learned about her needs. But by the time she knew what she wanted from a man, Rick had packed his bags for a gig in Seattle, leaving behind the divorce papers, their apartment lease and an ocean of emotions she'd only just emerged from.

But now she had a whole week off and a magazine detailing a city full of possibilities.

Benny leaned over the wooden bench to peek over her shoulder. "So, what are you planning to do when Athens closes?"

Ari turned the page of the magazine, intrigued by another sultry photo shot in a cell at Alcatraz. *Talk about bondage.*

She glanced up to see if Benny had noticed, but

his eyes were back on the line, his hands working the brake and bell with practiced grace.

"We'll be closed for over a month, but I only have a week for vacation. I'm not letting those contractors tear out one nail unless I'm watching."

Benny shook his head and clucked his tongue. "You can't be there all the time. Girl as young and pretty as you shouldn't be cooped up in that restaurant as much as you are. You need to get out. See the city. Enjoy being young while you can."

Ariana folded the next page over, her breath catching at the image of nude lovers immersed in the mineral baths in nearby Napa Valley. She'd never been to Napa. Not once. And by the looks of the photo, she was missing a lot more than wine.

"Sounds like a plan," she answered. "I've got one week to experience San Francisco. Think that's enough?"

Benny laughed heartily, the booming sound coming from his belly. The straining cables beneath the street, the heartline of old San Francisco seemed to chuckle right along with him.

"With the right man, a woman can experience the world in one night."

Ariana laughed in response, but privately mulled his words over, allowing her romantic side to believe Benny knew what he was talking about—that there was a man out there for her. One completely enamored with her. One who would put her pleasure, her satisfaction, before his needs. No, her pleasure and satisfaction would *be* his needs.

She wanted a sexy, uninhibited, confident man who would show her the soul of the city and the depths of her desires. And then, at the end of the week, he would fade away as if he'd never existed, leaving her with a lifetime of scorching memories to heat her through the cool San Francisco nights.

Without warning, the quixotic fantasy was slapped out of her head. Her hat tumbled onto her lap and she scrambled to catch it and the magazine before they flew off the car. Adjusting her backpack, she grinned wryly at the long tube that had just hit her—and at her own fanciful interlude. Such a dream lover didn't exist…in her experience. She had no men at all in her life except for Ray, the restaurant's day manager, who was happily married and treated her like a sister; her uncle, Stefano; the majority of her wait staff; and, of course, her customers.

Customers.

One in particular.

Benny slowed the cable car to pick up a trio of laughing coeds, then made the turn at Jackson Street for the brief ascent to Hyde, up toward the fancy houses on Russian Hill. Toward the place where she'd heard *he* lived.

He being one Maxwell Forrester. A customer.

But not just any customer. The customer she lusted after. The customer who'd shown up in one too many of her fantasies as of late, even though they'd exchanged no more than twenty-five words in the past year, not including, "Would you like lime in your club soda?" or "The crab pasta is particularly good today." He'd become a regular at Athens by the Bay, though one she'd wisely kept a distance from.

He possessed too much potent male power for a woman like her, at first reeling from a divorce and then determined to make her own way without any distraction from her goals. And Maxwell Forrester most definitely distracted her.

He jogged into the restaurant every morning for coffee before finishing his run to his office somewhere in the Embarcadero. Luckily, since she usually came in around two o'clock to handle the afternoon and evening crowds, she'd only seen him in the mornings on rare occasions. His sleepy, bedroom eyes and barely combed-through hair did a number on her senses each and every time. Not that seeing him after a long day at work was any better. He often jogged back from his office, in sweatpants and a windbreaker that were just ratty enough to mold to his broad shoulders and lean thighs, and just designer enough to remind her that he was out of her league.

She didn't know much about him—he was wealthy, did something in the real estate business and lived in Russian Hill. Ordinarily, she wouldn't even see him again until the restaurant reopened sometime at the end of next month.

Ordinarily.

Except that if fate was on her side… She checked her watch, shifting the magazine so she could activate the blue light. He might still be at the restaurant. The private party, a wedding-rehearsal dinner, had been booked at Athens by the Bay by Maxwell Forrester's friend, Charlie—another regular customer, but one she'd gotten to know a bit better. Charlie had worked with her to plan tonight's dinner, using their one-on-one meetings to casually drop the information that Max would be his best man at his upcoming wedding.

Charlie Burrows had all the subtlety of a barge. The groom-to-be made no secret that he thought Max and Ari should get to know each other better. Until she and Charlie had met yesterday to finalize the plans, Ari interpreted Max's cool friendliness toward her as a hint that he'd also heard Charlie's matchmaking arguments and wasn't interested.

But during their last meeting, Charlie had claimed that her assumption wasn't true. He'd never encourage Max to date anyone since his pal hated fix-ups. Unfortunately, Charlie was a horrible liar and Ariana sensed that there was something in his claim that didn't ring true.

But completely focused on her goals, Ariana had waved away Charlie's suggestion. She didn't need a date with anyone but her architect and her loan officer, and those were strictly business.

Of course, now all the blueprints were authorized and the financing was signed, sealed and delivered. She had to face the fact that she had a whole empty week ahead of her, a fascinating city all around her and an ignored libido driving her crazy.

Suddenly, crazy didn't seem so bad—and it definitely wasn't out of place in San Francisco. She fanned through the article, witnessing once again what this amazing, charming, insane city had to offer—with the right man and the right attitude.

MAXWELL FORRESTER SHOVED his platinum credit card back into his eelskin wallet and shrugged over the cost of his and Madelyn's wedding-rehearsal dinner. He had more than enough money to cover the expense, but growing up poor had saddled him with a frugal nature he constantly battled. A day didn't pass when he didn't remember going to bed hungry, knowing the food stamps had all been used, all too aware even at the age of ten that if he wanted so much as an extra peanut butter sandwich, he'd have to go out and earn it himself.

As expected of a man in his current financial position however, he'd told Charlie, his best man, to spend whatever was necessary to make the evening elegant for Max's future bride, their families and wedding party. He should have known better than to hope Charlie, Madelyn's favorite cousin and Max's best friend, would even think of capping his spending.

"You ready to go?"

"It's early yet," Charlie scoffed. "You've got one more night of freedom and you want to call it quits at—" he pulled his sleeve back to read his watch "—midnight?"

Charlie's argument lost some of its punch when even he realized that it was indeed late, what with the wedding less than twelve hours away.

Eleven hours, to be exact, Max realized. Not twelve. Not a minute more than eleven. Once he said, "I do," he'd be stuck with his decision to marry Madelyn. He shrugged away the thought. He wouldn't be any more stuck tomorrow than he was today. Max had already made a promise to Madelyn that was just as binding as a wedding vow. And though he considered himself an arrogant, driven son of a bitch who sought financial gain over just about anything else, he'd never break a promise to a friend.

"Marriage to Madelyn isn't a threat to my freedom," Max grumbled. He wasn't lying. Madelyn couldn't be a threat to his freedom when he'd really never had any in the first place. Max was a prisoner of his ambitions—he'd accepted that fact before he turned sixteen. But tonight the reality really rankled, partly because he was tired of this conversation with

Charlie, and partly because as he scanned the crowd in the barroom off to the left, he saw no sign of a Greek fisherman's cap bobbing behind the bar—or more specifically, the exotic dark-haired beauty who wore it.

"That's only because you don't know what freedom feels like, tastes like." Charlie grabbed his jacket from behind the chair, but slung it over his shoulder instead of putting it on, a sure sign that he wasn't ready to go. "You should leave that office of yours every once in a while—and not to jog through a city you don't see or to show a property you don't appreciate as anything but a potential sale. Heck, you and Maddie barely even date each other!"

Max attempted to tear his gaze out of the bar before Charlie noticed, but he wasn't quick enough. Charlie's grin annoyed him all the more.

"I don't want to hear this, Charlie. Madelyn is your cousin. You should be supportive of our marriage. It's what she wants."

Charlie grabbed Max's arm and tugged him into the bar. "Maddie is not just my cousin. She's my *favorite* cousin. She's the one person in the whole snooty family who didn't write me off when I flunked out of Wharton or when I decided to try my hand at acting before I moved back home. I owe her." He forced Max onto a bar stool and waved at the carrot-topped, college-age kid tending the bar. "She introduced me to you, didn't she? Got you to give me a try selling real estate. And who was your top agent last year? For the third time? Who's helping you become a millionaire more than any of the Yalies or finishing-school lovelies who show your listings?"

Max glanced back at the door, knowing he should

leave. He needed sleep. At least when he was sleeping, he wasn't thinking. And tonight, he didn't want to think. He'd promised Madelyn Burrows that he'd become her husband. They'd been friends since college. She'd helped him take the coarser edge off his Oakland habits, teaching him about designer clothes and fine wine and which fork to use at the country-club dinner. He'd repaid the debt by giving her a shoulder to cry on when she broke her engagement to P. Howell Matthews, her parents' handpicked son-in-law. She'd wept, not because she'd loved the guy, but because her parents had treated her like a mass murderer rather than a woman scared to death of choosing the wrong man.

So instead, she chose a friend, her best friend. He and Madelyn shared a love for jogging and natural-istic art, and they both appreciated old buildings—she saved them, he sold them. They also had a mutual desire to marry for reasons other than love.

Max had nothing against love. In fact, he admired the emotion. Revered it, even. His parents loved each other, and they loved his footloose brother, Ford, and Max unconditionally and with all their hearts. But love hadn't paid the rent on their tired Oakland apart-ment. Love hadn't kept his father from working twenty-hour days driving a cab. Love had only mar-ginally helped his mother endure the frustrations of teaching six-year-olds how to read and write when most of them were more concerned with getting their one, state-subsidized lunch, usually their only decent meal all day.

Love hadn't been enough to keep his family to-gether when his father was shot on the job. Unable to work, John and Rhonda Forrester had shuttled their sons from resentful relative to resentful relative. Eventually, the family had reunited, but the result was Max's single-minded pursuit of wealth and, over time, power, which had led him directly to the eve of a marriage that had nothing to do with love at all.

And he wouldn't even go into the havoc the emotion caused his brother. Ford was the most easygoing, likable man on the face of the planet, but he fell in and out of love quicker than Max unloaded a waterfront foreclosure. His younger brother had absolutely no idea what real love was about, and this was one lesson his big brother wasn't qualified to teach.

Max was, however, certain of only one immutable fact—love was fine and good for people willing to sacrifice and suffer for it, but he preferred to pursue success and financial satisfaction. Romance was a distraction. Until he'd met Maddie in college, he'd considered dating an unnecessary expense. Then she'd introduced him to her friends, girls with rich fathers and boundless connections. He'd dated the ones he liked, but drew the line at emotional involvement. So after graduate school, when Madelyn had suggested they "date" to keep her parents from fixing her up with another son of the country-club set like P. Howell Matthews, Max agreed. The ruse was born and had lasted all these years.

Madelyn was a pal. She understood his desire to make all of San Francisco forget that he was once a poor kid from Oakland—that now he was a force to be reckoned with in the lucrative business of buying and selling the most valuable properties in northern California. The marriage thing was more than he had bargained for, but Madelyn insisted the deal would work out for both of them.

Married to a Burrows, Max would have every door in San Francisco opened wide to him. Her father, her grandfather and her great-grandfather before him had all been prominent bankers with ties to every section of the diverse San Francisco community.

For Madelyn, the trade-off wasn't so clear—at least, not to Max. She claimed that marrying him would not only appease her parents, but the union would give her more clout with the wealthy matrons who financed her building restorations. Personally, he thought Madelyn deserved better—a man who loved her like a wife and would give her the passion she deserved. And he'd told her so on more than one occasion. But he owed her so much, cared about her so much, that when she begged him not to worry and to trust her decision, he'd gone along.

Like Charlie, he wasn't so sure he was doing the right thing. But he'd made his choice and he couldn't betray Madelyn now because of a bout of uncertainty.

"You're a real pal, Charlie, but Madelyn and I have discussed this over and over. I won't back out."

Charlie ordered two beers and shook his head. "You and Maddie are so blind. Neither one of you knows what you're missing. Lust, passion, desire. Marrying a friend is all well and good, but without the fire…" Charlie's words trailed off, his blue eyes glazed over.

Recently wed in Las Vegas to a woman he'd met in a suspicious jogging accident at Pier 39, Charlie was still high on the thrill of pure passion and uninhibited lust. Max paid the young bartender when he slid the beers in front of them, shaking his head at his friend, then glanced over his shoulder to see if anyone had overheard this unusual prewedding conversation.

That's when he saw her.

She entered through the front door between a departing party of four, stopping to shake hands with satisfied customers while Stefano Karas, the host for the evening, grabbed her backpack, shoved it at a nearby waiter and then ushered her into the bar.

Max turned aside. The last woman he needed to see tonight was Ariana Karas, with all her long, jet hair, ebony eyes and curves even her slimming black turtleneck, jeans and boots couldn't hide. She was exotic sensuality and alluring confidence all molded and sculpted into a compact package that made him fantasize about endless nights of sex. Nights that turned into days. And weeks. Maybe months.

Nothing but sex. No work, no money. No troubles.

He downed half his beer without taking a breath.

"Sex isn't everything, Charlie."

Charlie took a generous slurp of amber brew. "Oh, yeah? Says who? And I'm not just talking about sex, anyway. I'm talking about true love."

He sang the last two words as if he was joking, but Max knew Charlie well enough to realize his friend was a hopeless romantic. He was a free spirit who'd finally found some level ground with a job he was damn good at and a woman who obviously adored him, and vice versa.

"Yeah, well, if marrying your true love is so highly rated, what the hell are you doing here with me?" Max asked. "You should be home in bed with Sheri, not keeping me out till dawn."

Charlie chuckled, then quieted when Ariana

grabbed a black apron from the coatrack behind the bar.

"Sheri could use a little time to herself and you need me to talk some sense into you."

Max barely heard Charlie's explanation, more intrigued with watching Ariana flip the apron over her head before freeing her dark hair from beneath the pre-tied knot around her neck and fanning the luxurious length of it over her back. While wrapping the tie around her slim waist, she instructed the young guy who'd served their beer to cover the tables while she took over behind the bar. She tilted her hat at that jaunty angle that grabbed Max right at the center of his groin, and before he could look away, she captured his stare with a questioning glance.

"Something I can get you?" she asked.

Max sipped his beer, trying not to wince when the brew suddenly tasted strangely flat. "I'm fine, thanks."

She smiled, then made her way from one end of the bar to the other, checking on her customers, making small talk, replacing empty glasses and refilling snack bowls—all done with a quiet animation that made her both friendly and mysterious at the same time.

Max decided then and there that he was an idiot. He knew all about the lust Charlie lectured about. He'd been feeling the pull with growing intensity ever since he jogged into Athens by the Bay a little over two years ago and caught sight of the owner's niece helping a crew unload boxes from a delivery truck.

If he'd simply flirted with her and gotten to know her, he'd probably be long over this intense interest. Instead, he'd played it cool, ignored the attraction, turned away from her not-quite-shy, not-quite-inviting smiles that haunted him long after he'd run from the restaurant to the office, showered and parked himself behind his desk.

Now he was less than a day away from marriage, and the woman of his dreams was only an arm's length away.

"Hey, Ari," Charlie called, "how 'bout one of your specialty drinks for the road?"

"You driving?" she asked, grabbing a cone-shaped glass from beneath the bar.

Charlie grinned sheepishly. "Yeah, guess I am. Then how about making one for my old friend here?" He slapped Max on the shoulder. "He needs it more than I do anyway."

Ariana didn't laugh as Max expected, or as perhaps Charlie expected as well. Instead, she grabbed a collection of exotic liqueurs, one blue, one green, one amber, pouring the jewel-toned liquids into the glass on the edge of a knife, skillfully layering them with a clear, unidentified libation, so the colors barely mixed. After floating a layer of ruby-red grenadine on top, she moved toward them.

With confident grace, she lifted the drink in one hand and a bottle of ouzo in the other. She set the glass down in front of Max and without a word, swirled the ouzo over the grenadine. Focused on the glass, Ariana shielded her eyes from Max behind thick lashes, pressing the lips of her generous mouth into a pout that was focused and sexy as hell. When she finally looked up, meeting his thirsty stare straight on, he caught the glimmer of a smile twinkling in her night-black eyes.

He slid his hand forward, brushing his fingers over

the base of the glass. She crooked her finger around the stem. "Not so fast," she instructed, her voice breathy and low, but compelling all the same.

He questioned her with raised eyebrows.

She stepped up on the lower shelf behind the bar so she could lean forward and keep their exchange private. Max wanted to glance aside to see if Charlie or anyone else was watching, but he was slowly, surely, losing himself in the depths of her fathomless eyes. To hell with everyone else. She was just offering him a drink, not her body.

"This is my most special specialty." She skimmed her finger on the top layer of ouzo, careful not to disturb the rainbow of liqueurs underneath, then dampened the rim of the glass—precisely where his mouth would be when he took a drink. "I don't make it for just anyone."

Max's mouth dried. He moistened his lips with a thickening tongue. "I'm flattered."

"You should be. But you have to do your part, too." She dampened her finger again, but this time she touched the taste of ouzo to her lips. "This drink is called a Flaming Eros. Just like good loving, it takes two to make it hot."

Hot? Oh, yeah. Max was learning about heat very, very quickly. His collar grew tight around his neck. His body dampened with sweat. The perfectly starched shirt beneath his perfectly pressed jacket was starting to buckle.

"Makes sense," he managed to say.

Her fingers dipped into the pocket of her apron, then she slid her hand toward his, something small hidden beneath her palm.

Her phone number maybe? The key to her apartment?

He glanced down. A box of matches?

"So," she said, slightly louder, but still in a voice meant entirely for him, "care to light my fire?"

2

ARIANA SWALLOWED, savoring the ouzo she'd boldly stolen from his drink. She didn't know where the seductive move had come from; she wasn't exactly experienced with this sort of thing. But she'd spent enough time tending bar to watch some real pros work the room. Judging by the way Max Forrester's pupils expanded and darkened his eyes from pale jade to pine green, she wasn't doing half bad.

One week of freedom was all she had and, dammit, she wanted to spend at least one night with the man she'd lusted for since the first time she'd seen him. She'd never had an indiscriminate affair and, quite honestly, she wasn't starting now. Hell, since her divorce, she'd become the most discriminating woman in San Francisco. But Max Forrester exceeded even her high standards. He was gorgeous, had not just a steady job, but a full-fledged career and, according to Charlie, wasn't in the market for a wife.

She'd made the mistake of marrying her first lover and ended up waylaying her own goals and dreams in favor of his. Charlie claimed Max was a man of strong ethics, but he wasn't interested in long-term entanglements. And according to her own personal observation, he was potently sexy, inherently classy and, most important, he was undeniably interested.

Max took the box of matches from her, fumbling

slightly while sliding it open, and extracted a single match without spilling the others. She couldn't help but be impressed. She, being incredibly clumsy, had long ago taken to inviting her customers to remove a match rather than risk her sending them flying across the polished teak countertop. But she'd never made the offer with such a libidinous double entendre as "Care to light my fire?" Or if she had, the second meaning simply hadn't occurred to her before. That invitation to fire her personal hot spot belonged to Max and Max alone.

He shut the box, then poised the red-tipped end of the match against the flint. "My mother told me never to play with matches."

She leaned forward a little closer, unable to stop herself. Once she'd made the decision to seduce Charlie's best man, she wouldn't back down. Couldn't. The tide tugging her toward Max Forrester was more treacherous than the waves outside Alcatraz, and just as invigorating.

"She told you that when you were a little boy, right? Well, you're not a little boy anymore. Are you?"

He struck the match, inflaming the head, emitting a burst of smoke and sulfur that tickled her nose. She listed closer to him like a boat following the command of the waves. Amid the wispy scent of fire, she caught wind of his cologne. A musky blend of spices and citrus flared her nostrils and rocked her equilibrium.

He held the match toward her and she blinked, knowing she'd better get a hold of herself before she lit her Flaming Eros. She was already hot enough without adding third-degree burns.

She skimmed her fingers beneath his, brushing his hand briefly as she took the match away. The warmth of his skin was soothing. The look in his eyes was not.

She slid the glass back and skimmed the fire over the alcohol until the drink ignited in an impressive blue and orange flame. The bar erupted in applause and Stefano shouted last call. Ariana couldn't wait around to watch Max drink her concoction. She immediately had orders for three more. After sliding a small plate from beneath the bar to help him extinguish the flame and instructing him to do so before the fire burned through the grenadine, she grabbed his half-empty beer and her bottle of ouzo and moved farther down the bar.

She needed space. She'd probably only imagined the increase in her body heat the moment he'd stroked the match against the box, but she hadn't imagined the look of utter fascination in his eyes. How long had it been since a man looked at her that way? Since she'd *let* a man look at her that way without extinguishing his interest with a sharp phrase or quip?

Since her marriage? If she took the time, she could count it down to the minute. But she wouldn't. For the life of her, she was going to make sure that her marriage and divorce would cease to be a milestone in her life. Tonight would be the turning point.

She mixed the three flaming aperitifs, each more quickly than the last, letting the customer remove the match, but doing so much more silently and efficiently than she had with Max.

Care to light my fire? she'd asked. Trouble was, he'd done that a hell of a long time ago without even trying—simply by coming into her tiny wharfside restaurant one evening, ordering his beer with cool politeness and leaving a big tip—and then disappearing into the night. But he'd come back, nearly every weeknight. Never saying more than a few words, but speaking to her nonetheless—in sidelong glances, clandestine stares. Perhaps saying things she wasn't ready to hear.

Until tonight.

Little by little, the crowd thinned. The dining rooms were emptied, vacuumed and reset for the final breakfast crowd. Uncle Stefano stuffed the night's receipts into a vinyl bag then disappeared in the office to secure them in the safe so Ari could tally them later. In couples and trios, the customers went home. Waiters called good-night after scooping their tips from their pockets and tossing their aprons into the laundry basket by the kitchen.

But Max Forrester didn't move.

Ariana stuffed dirty glasses in the dishwasher, replaced all the bottles she'd used, stacked the mixers in the small refrigerator and wiped down the bar—all the while aware that Max hadn't left. Charlie had, sometime when Ariana hadn't noticed, and he'd done so without saying goodbye or thanking her for her help with his rehearsal dinner, which she thought odd but not surprising. The man *was* getting married in the morning. She was more than likely the last thing he had on his mind.

But obviously she was of interest to Max. Never before had he stayed late. Why else but for her? She was flattered. Terrified. Excited. He'd never flirted with her in the past, never so much as attempted to strike up a conversation beyond the day's specials. At the same time, he'd never been cold or dismissive.

Just standoffish, controlled. As if he chose to ignore their mutual attraction just as she did.

And yet, he'd lagged behind tonight. That had to mean something.

Ariana poured ouzo into a short shot glass and downed the fiery liqueur in one gulp. The licorice-tasting essence of anise coated her mouth, burned her eyes and her throat, but she needed the fortification. If Max hadn't left, it was, perhaps, because he'd read the subtle invitation in her eyes earlier, understood the hidden meaning in her question. Possibly she was about to be granted the wish she'd made while riding that cable car down Russian Hill, the bright moon shining just over the Bay Bridge, casting a hypnotic glow over the dark waters of San Francisco Bay.

She wanted to have an affair. This week and this week only. With Max Forrester and Max Forrester only.

She smoothed her damp cloth closer and closer to him at the bar. He didn't turn toward her. He sat, staring straight ahead, his gaze lost in the rows of bottles behind the bar. His Flaming Eros had barely been touched.

She glanced at the collection of whiskeys and bourbons and vodkas, wondering what held his attention so raptly.

"Hey, Max? You all right?"

Cautiously, she walked directly in his line of vision. There was a distinct pause before his eyes focused on her.

"Yeah. I'm great."

He blinked once, then twice. She saw him sway on his bar stool.

She shot forward and grabbed his hand. "No, you're not."

She glanced down at his drink again. He'd sipped maybe a quarter of the concoction and though her mixture was potent, she'd never seen anyone get drunk on just one. Maybe a little silly, but not ready to pass out.

"What did you drink tonight?"

She remembered clearing away a half-empty beer, but she had no idea what he'd had before she returned from her appointment with the architect.

She waited for him to answer and when he didn't, she asked again.

"What? Oh." He glanced down at his drink. "You made me this."

"No, I mean before. At dinner?"

He squinted as he thought. Remembering took more effort than it should have. He was drunk. Ariana rolled her eyes. *Great. Just great! I finally decide to have an affair with a guy and he's three sheets to the wind.* She recalled the distinctly forgettable experience of making love to her husband when he'd had more than his share of tequila after a gig in the Castro. Not an experience she'd *ever* want to repeat.

"Max, what did you drink at dinner?" she asked once more, losing her patience with the same speed as her attraction.

"Tea," he answered finally, nodding as the memory apparently became clearer and clearer. "We had tea."

"Long Island Iced Teas?"

Ariana hated that drink. She'd seen more than her share of inexperienced drinkers get sloshed thanks to the innocent-sounding name. Too bad there wasn't a drop of tea in the thing. Just vodka, gin, tequila, rum, Collins mix and an ounce of cola for color.

"Great, just…"

"No, iced tea. Unsweetened. With lemon."

As the truth of his claim registered, she stepped up on the lower shelf behind the bar again to look directly into his eyes. His pupils were huge—and passion had nothing to do with it. He was sweating more than he should have been. His jaw was slightly lax.

"You're sure? You've had nothing to drink but iced tea, half a beer and a few sips of my Flaming Eros?"

For a moment she thought she'd given him way too much to think about, but he managed to nod. "I feel kind of weird," he admitted. "I think I should…"

He pushed off his stool slowly, his hands firmly gripping the bar. If she hadn't been watching so closely, she might not even have seen him waver when his feet were firmly on the floor.

"You're not going anywhere."

Ariana scurried around the bar and caught him before he'd taken a single step toward the door.

"I can walk home," he reminded her, though he didn't pull away from the supportive brace of her shoulder beneath his arm.

"Oh, really? You make it to the door without my help and maybe, just maybe, I'll let you go." She had absolutely no intention of allowing him to go anywhere by himself, though her idea of seducing him was a great big bust. "You're not drunk, Max. Someone…someone in *my* establishment," she added with increasing anger, "slipped you a Mickey."

"A Mickey?"

She ignored his question, knowing that after a brief time delay, he'd understand. Someone had drugged him and it certainly hadn't been her. However, since the event had happened in her place, she could only imagine the trouble that could come just as she was about to break into the international restaurant scene. She'd heard about people using such deception at college parties. She'd read about the practice at raves and in dance clubs. But in a family-style restaurant? A neighborhood bar?

"Why?" he finally asked.

She shifted beneath his weight and guided him toward the door. "I have no idea." She called to the kitchen, which she suddenly noticed was quiet. She shouted twice more, then leaned Max against the hostess stand and ordered him not to move.

"Uncle Stefano? Paulie?"

The kitchen was empty. The floors were damp and the dishwashers steamed, but no one was around and the back door was bolted tight. She checked the office. Empty. Uncle Stefano and her chef, Paulie, never left without saying goodbye and making sure she had a ride home. It was nearly one o'clock and the last cable car left the turnaround at 12:59.

As she grabbed her backpack from behind her desk, removing the architectural plans and placing them atop the file cabinet, she wondered if Uncle Stefano had seen Max lingering in the bar and assumed she had plans for the night. She didn't know why he'd make such a ridiculous assumption except that, this time, he might have been right. And he had been hounding her about dating again, even agreeing with Charlie that Max made a good potential suitor. Perhaps Stefano thought she'd finally taken him up on his advice.

"Looks like it's up to me to take you home." She closed the office light and grabbed the keys.

Max shook his head, staggered then steadied himself to catch his balance. "Just call me a cab."

Ariana glanced at the phone, frowning. Yeah, a cab could get him home—he supposedly lived only a few blocks away. But what would happen in the morning when Maxwell Forrester, San Francisco real estate and power broker, woke up with a severe headache, possible memory loss and other unpleasant side effects? What would happen when he realized that she could be held culpable for his condition, even if no one who worked for her was involved? She didn't know how mad he'd be, but she imagined herself in his place and didn't like the picture that came into focus.

Negative word of mouth would be the least of her worries. He could call the press, file a lawsuit. If she lost her liquor license, even for the briefest time during an investigation, her business would be dead in the water. She'd invested in the reopening every asset she and her uncle held. She couldn't risk what had happened to Max—though through no fault of her own—jeopardizing her future.

She'd planned to take Max home tonight. No sense in changing the blueprint of her original plan this late in the construction.

"If we hurry, we can make the last cable car. Your place is..."

She moved to slip her arms beneath his again, but this time he caught her off guard. With one hand balanced on the hostess stand, he used the other to brush a strand of hair from her cheek. The friction of his fingernail against her skin was not unlike the lighting of the match. Heat flared where he'd touched her, so gently, so softly and yet with a pyrotechnic flash of instantaneous desire.

"Ariana," was all he said, four syllables on a deep-throated breath scented with anise, teasing her skin, fanning the flame she'd not so effectively tamped down just moments before. "I don't think I've ever said your name before," he said, curling the strand behind her ear, skimming her suddenly sensitive flesh as he thread his fingers into her hair.

She blinked, wondering if the mystery drug was the reason for his sudden interest, and if it was, wondering if she cared.

"I like the way you say it," she admitted, liking also the feel of his hand bracing her neck, his chest pressing closer and closer to hers so that the edge of his tie skimmed across her nipples. Her breasts tingled. Her breath caught. His arousal pressed through his slacks, taunting her. In the morning, he might not remember ever wanting her.

And again, she wondered if she cared.

"You're incredibly beautiful, Ariana. I've wanted to tell you that for a long time."

"Why didn't you?" she asked instantly, wincing when she realized that she might not want to know the answer.

His smile was crooked, tilted slightly higher on the left side. Still, the grin lacked the sardonic effect such an uneven slant might have on anyone else. Her insides clenched in a futile attempt to rein in her response—a cross between a magnetic pull and a bone-deep hunger for a man who was, in reality, a stranger.

Only he didn't *feel* like a stranger anymore, and he hadn't for a long while.

"Union Street," he answered.

"What?"

He hadn't answered her question, wasn't making sense.

He pushed away from her slightly. "You asked where I lived. On Union."

She nodded. Right. Get him home and to bed—though not at all in the way she'd originally intended.

"THIS IS INCREDIBLE!"

Max heard his voice echo beneath the clanging grind of the cable car, not certain he'd intended to share such an exuberant sentiment aloud. Yet when Ariana glanced over her shoulder and rewarded him with a smile that crinkled the corners of her eyes and flashed the whiteness of her teeth, he was glad he had.

"Haven't you ever ridden a cable car before?"

Max couldn't remember. He must have, but never like this. Against Ariana's wishes, he stood on the side step, one hand gripping the polished brass pole, the other aching to wrap around her slim waist and tug her close, back against him. So she could feel his hard-on. And know he wanted her.

And God, he wanted her.

So what was stopping him? He was sure there had been some reason at some time, but he couldn't remember and he certainly didn't care. The crisp San Francisco night air, clouded with a late-night fog, trailed through her nearly waist-length hair and fluttered the glossy strands toward him. The tendrils teased him with a scent part exotic floral, part crisp ocean—and all woman.

Without thought, he did as he desired, slipping his hand around her waist and stepping against her full and flush.

She stiffened slightly and nearly pulled away.

''I want to hold you,'' he said, beginning to accept that simple thoughts and simple explanations were all he could manage while intoxicated by whatever she'd said someone had put in his drink. He doubted her claim anyway. She had drugged him all right, but no pharmaceutical agent was involved.

She didn't protest when he curled his right arm completely around her waist, careful to remember that he had to hang on to the cable car with his left. His brain was fuddled, but his heightened senses compensated for his total lack of control. He fanned his fingers across her midsection. The texture of her ribbed shirt felt like trembling flesh. When he brushed his fingertips beneath the swell of her breasts, her back firmed, then relaxed, then pressed closer against him.

He dipped his head to whisper in her ear, ''I want to touch you.''

The cable car rocked and shimmied to a brief halt. A clanging bell blocked her reply, if she'd made one, but when the car moved again, she turned around and traded her handhold on the brass pole for a firm grip around his waist.

''Where?'' she asked.

She'd pulled her cap low and tight, so the dark brim pushed her bangs down to frame her large eyes. She bent her neck back to see his face, exposing an inviting curve of skin from the tip of her chin to the sensual arc of her throat.

His mouth felt cottony, but the desire in her eyes spurred a moisture that made him swallow deep. He ran his slick tongue over his lips and when she mirrored the move herself, his blood surged.

"Where will you touch me?" she asked again.

He blinked, a thousand thoughts racing through a brain too thick to harness them. The mantra "location, location, location" played silently in his mind then drifted away. Every single place he wanted to touch her—her lips, her throat, her shoulders, her breasts, her belly and beyond—seemed too intimate, too private to speak aloud.

He'd just have to show her.

He shook his head, grinning when his dizziness sent him swaying. She gripped him even tighter, giving him an excuse to dip his hold lower, over the swell of her backside, another place he most desperately wanted to touch with his hands and lips and tongue.

Max decided then and there that he had to accept his current limitations. As he had his entire life, he had to work with his immediate circumstances and the most basic skills at his disposal. His ability to speak was severely hampered. Forming a complex thought was out of the question. But he still had his instincts—natural, unguarded responses to basic, inherent needs. Hers and his.

"I'm going to touch you wherever you want me to."

Her smile was tentative, a little surprised and entirely fascinating—as if he'd said something that shocked her.

"What if that doesn't mean what you think it does?"

He shook his head. Processing that puzzle of a

comment was impossible in his condition. He didn't even consider trying.

"Whatever that means, I'm game. I'm in no condition to be in charge tonight. You're going to have to tell me what to do."

She chuckled. The sound was warm and deep and soothing like the liqueurs she'd poured in his drink, like the passions he'd kept in check for way too long.

"You may regret that," she quipped.

Somehow, he doubted he'd regret anything about tonight, especially when the cable car slowed at Union Street and she jumped off the car and crooked her finger into his waistband to tug him to follow. So what if someone had supposedly doctored his drink, making his mind so fuzzy he had a hell of a time remembering his address? So what if some crucial reason, currently out of reach, existed why he shouldn't let this incredibly sensuous woman take him home?

But no thought, no logic, no amount of reason could override the surge of power he felt even as she fairly dragged him up the sidewalk. He was going to make love to this mysterious woman with the sassy black hat.

Just as soon as he remembered where the hell he lived.

3

ARIANA SLID HER HAT off her head. Her backpack came down off her shoulder with it, but she held tight to the strap so it didn't touch the polished marble floor. She wasn't exactly a rube from some hick town, but standing in Maxwell Forrester's living room certainly made her feel like one. She'd expected wealth, not sheer opulence.

Everything was white. Pure white. The carpet, the furniture, the walls. Do-not-step-on-or-touch-me white. Glass cases of crystal sculpture reflected sparkling rainbow prisms, but the color was icy, precise. Only Max, a mass of gray and brown and flesh tone who shuffled in front of her before he flopped on the couch, shedding shoes and jacket and tie along the way, warmed the room with subtle invitation.

"Could you dim the lights? I had no idea I'd installed three-hundred-watt bulbs in my living room."

Ariana grinned. Filthy-stinking-rich or not, Max was in bad shape and needed her help. They'd walked nearly three blocks to his house and, with each step, the playfulness he'd enticed her with on the cable car had begrudgingly faded away. Right now he was in no condition to tell her where the light switch was, never mind detailing how and where he was going to seduce her. Maybe things were working out for the best. She would dim the lights, make sure he was comfortable and get the heck out of Dodge before she made a huge mistake.

But first she had to find the light switch. She searched fruitlessly, soon realizing that when they'd first come in, Max hadn't flipped any switches. He'd opened the door, they'd walked in and, snap, the lights had flared to life.

Oh, great. A house that was smarter than she was.

She backed up in the foyer and reluctantly laid her ratty leather backpack in the corner closest to the door and propped her hat on top, running her fingers through her windblown hair while she scanned the wall for a control panel that simply had to exist.

"Ariana? Are you still here?"

His voice was a mere whisper, but the sound still stopped her, warmed her—frightened the hell out of her. There was no mistaking the sound of hope mingling with the possibility of utter disappointment if she didn't answer, if she'd abandoned him in his glittering marble palace.

She found the switches behind a thick drape and slid the controls until the recessed lights shone like subtle moonlight rather than like the outfield at Candlestick Park.

"I'm here. Is that better?"

He'd removed his arm from across his eyes, then slid his elbows along his sides and propped himself up. "Now I can't see you."

She remained in the foyer, her boots firmly planted. "What's to see?"

The only thing coming in clear to her was the fact that she couldn't seduce Max Forrester. Not tonight. Maybe not ever. And she couldn't let him seduce her. Could she? She must have lost her ever-lovin' mind.

She obviously didn't belong here—with him—even temporarily. She was just a middle-class Greek chick trying to make a name for herself in the big city. He lived in a world she didn't understand and, therefore, couldn't control.

This was all a very big mistake.

"I said I'd get you home safe and sound. I should—"

"Don't leave."

For a man muddled by an unknown substance, he could issue a command with all the authority of a mogul, yet all the vulnerability of a man lost in a foreign land. She couldn't leave him—not, at least, until she was certain he'd be okay.

Somewhere between leaving the restaurant and sprinting to catch the last cable car, the desire that had deserted her when she thought he was merely drunk had crept back under her skin. The mystery substance made him dizzy, yes, but it also loosened his tongue and his inhibitions. The way he teased her on the ride, touched her, innocently and yet with utter skill, fired her senses and fed her fantasies.

If she forgot about the million-dollar town house, the imported sculptures, the computer-controlled light switches and focused only on the man, the possibility of making love to him didn't seem so impossible. Just…simple. Elemental. A fact of life in the wild, sexy city they called home.

Still, she held back, even while her mind said, *This is it.* Her chance of all chances to step onto the snowy carpet, shed her own jacket and make her fantasies come true. Heck, Max was already in a semireclined position. He'd already detailed several delightful means to "get to know each other better." How hard could a seduction be at this point?

But even if he wasn't drunk, he was, technically, "under the influence." If and when she and Max explored their mutual attraction, she wanted no regrets—from either of them.

"You don't know me, Max."

His grin lit his face, contrasting against the shadows all around him. "I'd like to remedy that."

His smile wavered at the same time as his balance. He slid his arms down, plopping back onto the cushions of the long couch and letting out a deep-throated groan. "Just my luck. I have the most beautiful woman in San Francisco standing in my doorway and I'm too dizzy to seduce her."

She laughed at the wry turn in his voice—until his words actually sunk in. Those drugs sure were powerful. The most beautiful woman in San Francisco?

She crossed her arms over her chest. Doubt and hope clashed in a war that resulted in her usual sarcasm. "You don't get out much, do you?"

He turned his head on the leather cushion. "Ariana, come closer. I'm in no condition to attack you, if that's what you're afraid of."

"I'm not afraid," she insisted, straightening her backbone, crossing her arms tighter and nearly stamping her foot on the tile. She wasn't afraid of anything, or anyone. Except, perhaps, of herself...with Max.

He shook his head and chuckled. The sound, like warm molasses, sweetened her indignation into humor, despite her preference to remain offended and aloof. Safe.

"I've seen you toss men twice my size out of your bar when they've gotten obnoxious. I didn't think

you'd be afraid of me, particularly not when I'm seeing two of you.''

She tugged on her lower lip with her teeth and
released her arms to her sides. Just as Charlie had
told her, just as she suspected from her own obser-
vations and brief interactions, Max was a man she
could trust. Trouble was, she didn't trust herself.

She hadn't factored in his natural charm and in-
stinctive warmth when she flipped through the pages
of that magazine and imagined Max making love to
her in all those exotic locales in the city. What if,
after a night of hot sex, she wanted more? What if
sating this particular hunger only whetted her appe-
tite? Would she be able to walk away? Would she
have the chance? The courage?

''Can you see the Golden Gate from here?'' she
asked, pointing at the bank of clear-glass windows in
Max's dining room that faced the Bay, delaying her
decision if only a moment more.

Glancing over her shoulder at her backpack, she
thought about the magazine. She hadn't read the
whole article, but she remembered one of the romantic settings was an incredibly posh hotel suite over-
looking the Bay. The view of the Golden Gate glit-
tered to the northwest, the Bay Bridge gleamed
somewhere farther southeast, and the lighthouse at
Alcatraz flashed at the center. The couple made love
against a wall of windows with an unhampered view
of the city.

''The best view is from the third floor, my balcony.
I would show you...''

She lifted her foot to step on the carpet, then sat
instead and unzipped and removed her boots.

''You're not in any condition to climb stairs.

Maybe I should make you some coffee." She lined up her shoes by the door. "Point me in the direction of the kitchen and I'll brew a pot."

"I think I've had enough of your libations," he answered.

"I could just leave—" she teased.

He hoisted an arm in the air from where he lay stretched full length on the sofa and pointed to her right. "Through the archway and up the stairs. I'm not sure where the coffeemaker is."

She stepped onto the carpet, sinking nearly an inch, the plush softness of the flooring cushioning her stockinged feet as she walked. "I know my way around a kitchen."

"What about bedrooms?"

She stopped beneath the archway. Damn, but anything the man said sounded like a come-on, with that deep, raspy voice of his. She was suddenly glad they hadn't exchanged more than a few dozen words over the past two years or she'd have ended up in his bed a long time ago.

Nevertheless, so long as he was asking about bedrooms, she might as well find out exactly what he had in mind. She stepped slowly to the edge of the couch. Leaning forward, she braced her hands on the armrest on either side of his bare feet.

"What do you want to know about bedrooms?"

A lock of her hair fell forward, brushing over his toes. His lips opened as if to answer, but no words came out.

"Max?"

"Sweats. I could use a pair of sweats."

She nodded and smiled, then headed back toward the kitchen. "I'll see what I can do."

Again, the room lit up the moment she entered, and like the living room, the light gleamed off polished white surfaces. She searched first for the coffee and a pot to brew it in. Then she'd think about his bedroom.

His bedroom. Dangerous territory.

She had no idea if his request for sweatpants had been what he'd originally intended to ask for, but she didn't doubt that he'd chosen a safer topic by requesting the change of clothes. He had no way of knowing that her knowledge of bedrooms was essentially limited to the art of sleeping in one. Her sexual experiences from her marriage—more specifically, the first few weeks of her marriage—seemed a lifetime ago rather than just a few years. She vaguely remembered the sex between her and her husband to be wild in the beginning, but even then she hadn't had much of a reference from which to draw comparisons.

She'd married as a virgin, sheltered by a family and community who clung to strict codes of feminine conduct—codes she'd wanted to rebel against for a very long time, but hadn't had the courage until her nineteenth birthday. She'd packed her bags and bought her plane ticket without telling a soul. Only after she was securely on her way to live with Uncle Stefano in San Francisco did she call her parents from her layover in Atlanta. She hadn't wanted a big scene. She just wanted to experience life on her own, with her own rules.

Her first goal had been to meet some gloriously sexy man and have a whirlwind affair. And she'd actually met Rick while waiting for a cab at the airport. A musician with his guitar slung over his shoulder, shaggy blond hair and kind eyes, Rick had captured her sensual imagination with his first smile. He'd offered to share the cab, and on the twenty-minute ride to the Wharf, they'd chatted and laughed and flirted and fallen in love.

But it was the wrong kind of love. The kind of love that didn't last. The kind of love exchanged by people who had little in common but lust. The kind of love that destroyed her second goal—the restaurant she finally now had just within her reach.

She'd learned the difference between lust and love the hard way, even if she'd never really experienced the latter emotion firsthand. Working with Stefano and Sonia, even intermittently before her aunt's death, taught her that what she'd had with Rick wasn't even close to what she deserved. She'd confused lust and love once. She certainly wouldn't do so again.

After her divorce, she realized that maybe if she'd just slept with Rick a few times before the quick wedding ceremony at the courthouse, the magic might have worn off long enough for her to see that they weren't in the least compatible. His goals included fame, fortune and, ultimately, a move to Nashville where he now lived and performed. At the time, her only goal had been independence, complete freedom from her family and the chance to run her own business. Marriage pretty much canceled both out. She'd inadvertently traded one controlling force for another. Once Rick was completely out of her life, she'd realigned her goals, recaptured her dream of being in charge.

But her personal goals? Her private wants? Until tonight, until she'd glanced through that magazine, she hadn't allowed herself the luxury of those. Such an unattainable, dangerous dream could spin her in the wrong direction yet again. So she limited her fantasies to when she was sleeping, or when the romance and rattle of the cable cars worked a sly magic on her tired, lonely heart.

Until tonight, she hadn't had time for a lover, even a temporary one. She worked twelve to sixteen hours at the restaurant every day of the week. Her one indulgence to pampering herself was practicing tai chi with Mrs. Li, her landlady, and sharing an occasional tea and conversation with the women who gathered in the shop below her apartment.

If she'd learned one thing about men in the past eight years—heck, in her whole life—it was that they demanded attention. Men like Max Forrester needed either a dutiful, socially acceptable wife to cater to his every need, or taffy-like arm candy—sweet and pliable to his slightest whim. She couldn't allow herself to be either. She'd end up investing herself in her lover rather than in her own future. She'd done it before and damned if she'd do so again.

She found and set up the coffeemaker, impressed at the organization she found in the cabinets and drawers. Either Max was completely anal-retentive or he had an incredibly efficient housekeeper. Probably a combination of both.

While the coffee perked and popped, emitting an enticing aroma that reminded her that she'd had nothing to eat since lunchtime, she decided to search his bedroom for the clothes he wanted. The staircase she'd taken to the kitchen continued upward and she figured the master suite more than likely took up the greater portion of the top and final floor.

The house reacted to her entrance by engaging the

lights again, but this time the glow was slight from a single lamp at the bedside. The lampshade's geometrically cut, stained-glass design reflected hues of gold and amber, with a touch of ruby red that reminded her of fire. Where the bottom floor reflected cold class and wealth, his bedroom was all male heat and casual comfort, though the lingering smell of money still teased her nostrils like aged wine or hand-rolled tobacco.

The walls were paneled with rich wood—not the cheap stuff her father had in his den back home, but thick, carved planks of teak that reminded her of the opulence of a castle—the sort of room a knight or duke might entice his lover to. The paintings, from what she could make out with the individual lights above them unlit, captured outdoor scenes—listing cutters with fluttering sails on an angry ocean, a majestic lake surrounded by snowcapped mountains, a single aquamarine wave rolling in on a honey beach.

And the bed—the California king, with a simple sleigh headboard and footboard—was huge and, most likely, custom-made. The fluffy comforter, half-dozen pillows and coordinating shams picked up the blues and greens from the paintings and swirled them with just enough gold to brighten the dark space to a subtle warmth. A pair of gray sweatpants had been tossed across the perfectly made and arranged linens. This was Max's room. The real Max. The Max she had wanted to seduce.

Truth be told, the Max she *still* wanted.

She grabbed the sweatpants, then thought to bring him a T-shirt as well. With a shrug, she carefully opened the drawers in his dresser, smirking when the top drawer yielded an interesting collection of party favors he'd obviously gotten from Charlie's bachelor blowout: a package of cheap cigars shaped like penises, chocolate lollipops sculpted like breasts, several foils of condoms with doomsday sayings about marriage printed on the packages.

She hadn't exactly planned and prepared for this evening's possible seduction, so in the interest of safe sex, she grabbed the square with the least offensive message and tossed it on the bed before resuming her search for a shirt. After grabbing one with Stanford emblazoned on the front, she moved to return to the kitchen, but stopped when she noticed the wall of heavy drapes facing the Bay. Curious after remembering his comment about the best view being from the third floor, she fumbled behind the thrice-lined curtains until she found the right button. One click and the window treatments slid aside, a mechanical hum accompanying her awed gasp.

The entire wall was a window—sliding glass doors, to be exact. Beyond was a tiled balcony almost entirely enshrouded in thick San Francisco fog. She couldn't resist a closer look. Tossing Max's clothes back onto the bed, she worked the locks with ease, then stepped into the mist as if entering a dream.

The air stirred with the breath of the Bay. An instant chill surrounded her, penetrating her clothing and dampening her hair. Her clothes drank in the moisture, making the cotton cool and clingy. Her nipples puckered beneath her turtleneck, rasping tight against her satin bra. She thought of Max, nearly passed out in the living room. Dizzy. Flirtatious. Sexy and charming and more potent than 120-proof rum.

Too bad he wasn't here when she needed him, when she just might be tempted to surrender to desire.

Tiny red lights blinked to the west, indicating the span of the Golden Gate. She strolled through the wispy fog until she approached the wall, surprisingly low—maybe three feet tall—that enclosed the patio. She kept a safe distance from the edge and closed her eyes, remembering the image in the magazine of the lovers on the bridge, right up against the railing. She superimposed her face on the woman again. And this time she did the same to the man, giving him Max's thick, dark hair, rugged square chin and gentle, probing fingers.

She saw them clearly. A man—*Max*. A woman—*her*. An undeniable desire, hidden by just a touch of fog. Tonight's mist was particularly thick for such a late hour—San Francisco fog usually rolled over the city around four o'clock and dissipated by midnight.

Yet nothing about this night was usual. Definitely not her. Not her uncontrollable desire for Max. Not the circumstances that brought her here or the consequences she'd face in the morning if she stayed.

She pursed her lips, realizing the consequences—a little embarrassment, perhaps a dose of discomfort in the morning light—were more than worth the price of living her fantasy, grabbing her dream with both hands and saying, "Yes! Now!" That strategy had paid off once when she'd taken over the operations at the restaurant. Had she not succumbed to her youth and married the first man she met at the airport, she might have been able to say the same about the day she bought her ticket to San Francisco and left her loving, but stifling, family behind.

"Yes. Now," she repeated aloud, trying the words on for size.

"Just tell me what you want."

His voice rolled over the tiles and through the thick fog like a warm blast of summer air. The contrast spawned a ripple of gooseflesh up the back of Ariana's neck, then crept beneath her turtleneck and played havoc with her skin.

She squeezed her eyelids tighter as the sensations rocked her balance, nearly unraveling her completely when Max's breath mixed with the fog and whispered into her ear.

''Tell me what you want. Anything, Ariana. Anything goes.''

4

"IS THAT A FACT?"

Her tone was saucy, despite the whimper begging to erupt from the back of her throat. She tamped down the sound of surrender with a thick-throated swallow and willed herself to remain in control. Acquiescence to the night—the passion, the mood, the man—should be resisted. She had to keep her wits. But she couldn't deny that this liaison would be more than a fantasy come true, more than a living dream.

The night. The fog. The man. The desire. Ariana knew without a doubt that what swirled around her at the ledge of the balcony was a gift, a once-in-a-lifetime twist of fate that she'd be a damn fool to refuse. If only he was thinking clearly!

Max stepped around, taking her hand and leading her to the ledge. His bare arm brushed against hers as he reached for the round, brass railing that edged the thigh-high brick wall enclosing his patio. Tan skin stretched tight over powerful arms and sinuous shoulders.

He'd removed his shirt. The sprinkle of tawny hair over his arms and across his chest prickled in the cool air. When the fog shifted, she realized he'd shed his pants on the way upstairs as well. He wore nothing but a thin pair of midnight-blue boxers, damp from the mist.

She tried not to allow her gaze to linger, but found her quest impossible. The shape of his erection, swathed in silk and taut with want, ignited a throbbing heat between her legs. A thrill skittered straight to the center of her chest.

She swallowed and rubbed her arms to ward off a shiver that had little to with the temperature. "Aren't you cold?"

He inhaled deeply, his chest expanding impressively. His muscles were distinct and smooth, honed from running and perhaps some weight lifting or rowing—the kinds of exercise a rich man used to mold his body for the torture of women like her.

"I like the cold. It's invigorating." He turned and sat on the low railing, his legs stretched leisurely outward. Plucking her sleeve with his fingers, he snapped the clingy material against her skin. "You should experience it for yourself."

A zing of awareness shot through her arm, but she found it hard to enjoy with him poised so precariously on the ledge. Her stomach clenched. A threatening whirl of dizziness danced at the edges of her eyes. God, she hated heights!

"That railing is awfully low, you should be…"

Max smiled and leaned completely backward. Ariana screamed and shot forward, grabbing both his arms and fully expecting both of them to tumble over. But a wall of clear, thick Plexiglas caught him before he rolled them off the three-story building. The shield vibrated from their combined weight.

The wall of his chest caught her, vibrations of a sensual kind rocked her to her core.

"Cool feature, huh? Lower wall, better view," he explained, slipping his arms around her waist and pulling her between his thighs and onto his lap. He was hard beneath her, hard all around her. Hard and male and dangerous. "But still completely safe."

Ariana decided then and there that men like Max Forrester shouldn't be allowed to use the word *safe* in any form. She shivered from the cold, from the pure, unadulterated lust coursing through her bloodstream and firing her every nerve ending. She panted to catch her breath.

"That was a cruel trick," she answered, forcing herself to look him in the eye.

His grin faded. "The cruel trick is you coming out here without me and leaving one of these on my bed for me to find when I came looking for you." He held the foil packet aloft. "An invitation?"

She arched an eyebrow. "A friendly reminder."

"I do remember that I promised to show you this view myself." He tugged her closer. The scent of sandalwood, enhanced by his body heat and diffused into the fog, assailed her. The result was a light-headed euphoria that made her hold him tight.

"And I promised to touch you wherever you wanted me to. Put those two promises together," he said, grinning at her impassioned grip on his arm, "and the experience will be absolutely unforgettable."

He swallowed deeply, and Ariana watched the bobbing of his Adam's apple and the undulation of his throat, fascinated.

"You say that now. But that drug can alter your memory."

"I don't feel drugged by anything but you."

Her chest tightened in response to his declaration. She couldn't see clearly in the dim lighting on the balcony, but Max certainly seemed to have control of his balance now, something he hadn't had earlier. Maybe the Mickey had lost some of its effect.

Anticipation warred with her uncertainties—sexual excitement battled with a lifetime's worth of repression and regret. She had every reason to believe that Max's desire was honest—true in a way that was elemental to a man and ideal for a woman like her. She could have him tonight, love him tonight, knowing they were both sating a desire born long ago and hidden for reasons that, right now, simply didn't matter.

What did matter was that in the morning she'd have an adventure to remember, a sensual liaison that would erase the erotic pictures from the magazine with images of delight so much more personal and real.

She grazed her hands upward from his elbows to his shoulders, kneading the thick sinew as she worked inward to his neck. For a man who reportedly wielded great power during the day, his muscles were now completely relaxed and pliant to her touch. His eyes, half-shut as she threaded her fingers into his hair, were focused entirely on her, seeming to see something fascinating, something no other man ever had.

She moved forward to kiss him, but his hands snaked from her waist to her elbows and stopped her.

"Wait," he ordered.

Confused, she instinctively pulled back from his grip. He released her, but stood and stepped immediately back into her personal space. She gasped and retreated. He shadowed her move.

"Don't bolt, Ariana."

"Why'd you stop me? This isn't a good idea."

"You were going to kiss me," he answered simply.

She bit her lower lip before replying. "And?"

"And you were touching me." He did as she did earlier, sliding his hands from her elbows to her shoulders, then massaging inward to her neck until his thumb teased the lobes of her ears.

"You didn't like it?" she murmured. She couldn't imagine how he wouldn't have. She was having a damn hard time keeping her eyes open and her moan of pleasure contained in her throat.

"I loved it, but that's not what tonight is going to be about."

"Huh?"

If a more intelligent response existed, Ariana couldn't summon it. Not with his scent, hot and male and potent, assailing her nostrils and his body heat defeating the night's chill like fire against ice.

"My brain has defogged. My balance is back. And if I remember correctly, I promised that if you stayed, tonight would be about you. Me pleasing you. Not necessarily the other way around."

She barely had time to register that he had just voiced her ultimate fantasy, when he lowered his head and brushed her lips with a teasing sweep. The sensation unleashed that imprisoned whimper, then several more as the kiss deepened, mouths opened, tongues danced. Before she realized it, Max untucked her shirt from her jeans and skimmed her belly with a light, exploratory touch.

Electric need surged through her. She jumped, startled and thrilled and excited, then grabbed his cheeks and pressed closer to force herself past her panic. Max wouldn't hurt her. Max would stop if she asked.

And she definitely didn't want to stop.

His lips stretched tight as he grinned beneath the

kiss. He unbuttoned her jeans and released the zipper, barely touching her in the process, which only stoked her hunger for more. She broke the kiss long enough to whip off her turtleneck, tossing it aside to disappear in the soupy mist swirling around them, then kissed him again. He led her backward until her calves bumped against an outdoor chaise lounge.

Pressing his hands on her shoulders, he guided her into the chair, following her down so that he knelt beside her. With intimate slowness, he eased her fully against the cushion, altering his kisses from bold and insistent to soft and scattered, touching her nose, her eyelids, her cheeks, her chin, lulling her into an anticipatory state where she held her breath and waited for his next touch.

When she finally opened her eyes, his grin was pure sin.

"Do you feel it?" he asked, his green eyes twinkling with some untold secret.

"Feel what? You stopped."

"Oh, honey—" he smiled as he removed her jeans, the denim rasping over the sensitive skin of her legs, leaving her wispy panties askew "—I've only just started. I meant the anticipation. Do you feel that?"

She nodded, rubbing her tongue-dampened lips together tightly. The fog kissed her bare legs. The chill made her shiver, but the sensation was nothing compared to the waves of want rocking her from the inside out.

"It'll only get better, I promise."

He tugged the denim off her ankles, then straddled the chair so he could attend to her bare feet. He massaged her arches and toes with a strong pressure that at first made her wince, then he kneaded softly until she sighed. She hadn't realized how tired her feet were. But with each press and swirl, his hands erased the ache of the workday and enhanced the bittersweet torment of unsatisfied need.

He inched upward, lifting her left leg and placing an anklet of wet-tongued kisses on her skin, followed by a seam of laving up her calf and behind her knee. She started to slip down the fog-slickened cushion. The plunging sensation made her grab the arms of the chair.

"Relax, Ariana. I won't hurt you."

"It's not that. I feel like I'm falling."

"You are. You're falling for me."

She shook her head, smiling at his sweet sentiment, but not surprised that he didn't understand.

"I'm afraid of heights," she admitted.

"Heights of passion?" His teasing tone and sparkling eyes drew her into his double entendre. He scooted forward another few inches, then draped her knee over his shoulder. She held her breath, watching, fascinated and vulnerable and thrilled, as he smoothed his hand from beneath her lifted thigh, down to her nearly bare bottom. Wordlessly, he grabbed an elongated cushion from a nearby chair and placed it behind her hips, securing her in the semi-lifted position. She grabbed the neck roll and slid it behind her head, assisting him as he arranged her body for his full view and complete attention.

"I wouldn't know about the heights of passion, Max," she admitted. She'd avoided them the same way she'd avoided climbing Coit Tower or walking the span of the Golden Gate. The possibility of plunging down, losing herself, was a real one she'd always meant to avoid. "Never really climbed them."

He shook his head. "A damn shame, beautiful woman like you." He tilted his head and kissed her knee. "That will change. I promise."

With a glance half skeptical, half intrigued, she surveyed the unusual position he'd sculpted her body into. Her knee remained draped over his shoulder and, with the pillows beneath her hips, he could see all of her, touch all of her while hardly moving.

"I can see that," she quipped.

He chuckled appreciatively, raking his fingers down the inside of her thigh. "This is San Francisco. We don't do things the conventional way here."

Ariana took a deep breath, swallowed the last of her ingrained apprehension and folded her arms behind her head. She concentrated on the sensuous trail Max blazed with his hands, up and down her leg, touching her but not touching her—promising intimacy with a wicked tease.

"So far, you're all talk," she said, biting her lip the moment her provocation lit his eyes with a fire she doubted she could contain.

"Talk can be good," he answered.

"Talk can be cheap."

One dark eyebrow tilted, along with the corner of his incredible mouth. "I don't buy cheap."

"You're not buying me," she answered, still grappling with the incongruity between her standard operating modes and this incredible dalliance with a stranger. The sensations, the heat emanating from his body to hers dulled reality, but couldn't erase it entirely, no matter how she tried.

He kissed her knee again and slid it down his arm so that she straddled his thighs. Scooting forward, he ran both hands up her legs and hips, spanning his fingers inward across her stomach then upward, lightly over her breasts to her neck. He unhooked her hands and pulled her forward until they sat, entwined, his mouth to her ear.

"There are some highs that can't be bought, even by men like me."

She gasped as he skimmed his fingers down her back and unhooked the back of her bra. The satin loosened as he drew the straps aside, one at a time, releasing her, revealing her. He tossed the lingerie aside, pressing his hands hotly against her shoulder blades so she arched toward him and he could look his fill.

"Care to borrow a little ecstasy with me?" he asked. His grin was part irreverent, part hopeful.

She could only nod.

He skimmed his hands up her sides and cupped her breasts.

"Tell me what you want," he said.

She licked her lips. "This."

Tracing a lazy circle with his thumbs, he skimmed the full circumference of her breasts, spiraling inward until he reached but didn't touch her nipples. Round and round and round he traced tight, grazing rings that never made contact with the sensitive centers, but eased them into a taut, hungry pucker that made her coo.

"Now what?"

"Kiss me."

"Your breasts?"

"Yes."

He glanced up and captured her gaze from her half-closed eyelids.

"Offer them to me," he said.

She blinked, uncertain. He took her hands and guided them up her own rib cage, until she cupped herself.

He met her stare with sweet challenge. "Offer them to me," he repeated.

She smiled and did as he commanded, lifting her breasts high and arching her back. She closed her eyes tight in anticipation, dizzy from the sensation of taking control of her own pleasure.

He didn't disappoint. Splaying his hands beneath her bottom, he lifted her the last inch he needed to take her fully into his mouth. His lips were cool from the breeze, his tongue hot, alternating between soft and stiff as he pleasured her with a sweet attendance to detail.

Max the stranger became Max her lover with each and every intimate kiss.

He cupped her with his hands, flicking his thumbs over her moistened flesh while his kiss wandered across her collarbones and up her neck. Their lips clashed in a hot, breathless battle. She touched him everywhere, down his back, up his arms. Fingers crashed through his hair, dipped into his boxers. Learned him as he learned her.

He lifted her as he stood, letting her feet touch the ground long enough to remove the last scraps of clothing between them, then he wrapped her legs around his waist as he carried her to the ledge.

Max set her down and turned her so her half-closed eyes could see the glorious view of the bridge and the Bay drifting in and out of the fog. Lights twinkled in the distance as he pressed against her back and enveloped her with his heat. The flashing lights appeared behind her heavy eyelids when he slid his hand down her belly through her dark curls to test her need.

He nestled his cheek to hers, stroking her gently with one hand, caressing a breast softly with the other. "Open your eyes, Ari. I promised to show you the view."

Swallowing deep, she managed to form a coherent sentence as her mind drifted in and out of utter ecstasy. "Don't wanna see. Mmm. Just feel."

He tugged her earlobe with his teeth. "Do both. Don't settle for less when you can have it all."

Have it all. Ariana grinned and forced her eyes open. Swirls of whitish gray fog shifted and drifted on the other side of the Plexiglas wall, allowing her glimpses of the city she hardly knew but loved anyway. The irony didn't escape her. She felt eerily the same about Max, a stranger who touched her with such tenderness, and who was slowly becoming her most intimate lover.

"Are you watching?" he asked.

The question may have been meant to distract her from the fact that he'd stepped away to put on the condom, but she felt his absence so deeply, she grew chilled.

When he returned, his first order of business was reigniting her warmth.

"I'm looking," she said, bracing her hands on the brass railing as he kissed and caressed her, rubbing her arms, nuzzling her neck, grinding his stiff sex against her bottom. "I'm not seeing much with this fog."

"Look closer," he whispered, touching her ear with his tongue.

She blinked and refocused, noticing with a gasp

that with the light bouncing out from the bedroom behind them and with the thick fog, their images were reflecting back from the Plexiglas like a bathroom mirror steamed from a hot shower. She could see his hands easing from her hips to her belly to her breasts. She watched, enthralled, as he plucked and stroked her. Electric sensations drew her lids down with a magnetic pull.

"I see you touching me. Feel you..."

Her voice drifted into the fog and disappeared as images, opaque and erotic, rode across her vision. He pressed closer, slipping his sheathed sex between her legs, teasing her with a gentle friction, while his hands tilted and guided her.

"Tell me what you want," he said again, and she couldn't imagine why.

"Make love to me," she answered.

"That's what I'm doing, sweetheart." His fingers dipped low. Jolts shook her.

"I'm going to come. Too soon."

Fighting the sensation was fruitless. Fruitless and senseless and entirely out of her control when his hands still stroked her, played her, building the madness to an unbearable peak.

"Not too soon. Don't fight me. Let me."

With the hand that wasn't driving her wild, he swept her hair over her shoulder so he could suckle her from the tip of her shoulder to the pulse at the base of her neck. His fingers probed deeper, stroked harder until the image she saw in the misty glass was a woman driven completely wild. She bucked, but he held her fast. She screamed, and he cheered her lack of inhibitions, demanded she hide none of her rapture.

Just when she started on the downward side of ecstasy, he pushed inside her, stretching her with one, slow thrust.

She gripped the handrail so tight, her fingers ached. She couldn't. Not again.

But when he smoothed his palms over her hips in lazy, gentle circles, she knew he would wait. And the wait would be worth her while.

"Max," she started, nearly breathless, completely unsure what she had to say to convince him that she'd never experienced something so incredible, something she most certainly wouldn't experience again until after a good night's sleep.

He caressed her softly, teasingly, up her sides, beneath her arms, then guided her arms upward, placing her hands firmly on the Plexiglas. She stared into her own diaphanous reflection. Even amid a cloud, the undiluted satisfaction in her eyes was impossible to miss.

"That's one way to enjoy the view," he whispered, wrapping his arms around her so he could love her breasts again. "Wanna try another?"

Ariana swallowed, forcing herself to inhale and exhale, forcing herself to accept that her body, her mind, her soul wanted this man inside her—wanted to share the incredible fantasy again and again and again in every way imaginable. The feel of him, slick and hard, taut and silky, penetrated her, enveloped her in a heat that was inherently pure, amazingly simple. Like a beating heart. Like a breathing soul.

"I trust you, Max," she admitted, not meaning to say it aloud, but glad when she did.

He stopped his sensual assault long enough to give her the sweetest, softest embrace, topped with a touch of a kiss on her cheek.

"I won't let you down."

5

"DID YOU GET IT?"

Jangling the change in his pocket, Leo Glass hooked the receiver of the pay phone beneath his chin. "Not exactly."

"What do you mean *not exactly?* Photographs are photographs. What did you do, put your thumb on the lens?"

Leo bit back the urge to tell the jerk on the other end of the line exactly what he could do with his condescending attitude. But he needed the cash the man was supplying. And the revenge wasn't so bad, either. "I'm not that stupid."

"Remains to be seen."

"I heard that!"

"I wasn't exactly whispering, was I? There's only an hour left. Did you get pictures of them or not?"

"I got 'em. But the damn fog..."

"They were outside? How disgusting." After a pause, the man snickered. "But interesting, for my purpose."

"Might have been, if you could *see* anything."

"So you didn't get the photograph?"

"I wouldn't say that. You can't exactly tell who's who, but the two figures in the shot are definitely doing something interesting on that balcony."

The next pause nearly drove him insane. Leo shook

his pockets again, annoyed at the sound of four quarters, two dimes and three pennies swirling around with nothing green to keep them company—at least, not yet.

Finally, the bastard with the cash to make his future easy gave him the answer he wanted.

"Bring them in, with the negatives. With the right spin, we might be able to use them to our advantage."

I TRUST YOU, MAX.

The voice, soft and feminine, was familiar, stirring a misty memory Max struggled to stay asleep to relive. The tone was deep, sultry, exotic. Impressions fleeted by. Abandon. Rapture. Release.

Freedom.

I trust you.

"Max?"

His eyelids snapped open at the crisp sound of his name, this time as real and strong as the sunlight streaming into his bedroom. Who left the drapes open? He never left the drapes open.

"Who?"

A figure stepped over to the window and pressed the button that drew the drapes closed with painful slowness. In the meantime, he fell back onto his pillow and laid his arm across his eyes until the sickening swirls of oranges and reds and purples dancing in his eyelids faded away.

"Are you okay? Max?"

"My head is pounding. My mouth feels like I swallowed a sheep," he answered to whoever the hell was asking the question. A woman. A woman he highly suspected he should know.

A woman with a sultry, exotic voice.

Her laugh was light and might have annoyed him under other circumstances. He pressed his hands against his temples, surprised to discover he *wasn't* wearing a football helmet that was two sizes too tight. Actually, he realized, drawing his arm aside, if her laugh didn't piss him off in his current misery, which it didn't, the buoyant sound probably never would.

The room was a cloud of shadows, but he felt her weight when she sat on the bed beside him.

"If you sit up, you can drink my special blend. It may not make you feel a whole lot better, but it most definitely won't make you feel worse."

Sit up. She may as well have asked him to shoot up the steepest part of Lombard Street on in-line skates.

"I can't move."

"What a shame. Your moves last night were incredible."

It may have been a while since he'd heard the distinctive purr of a woman just recently satiated and satisfied, but the molasses-sweet and sun-warmed sound was impossible to forget. He pushed his physical discomfort aside long enough to prop himself up on his pillows.

His eyes adjusted. The skylight in his bathroom threw just enough glow into his room to let him see what he was certain was a dream.

Ariana Karas? Offering him coffee? In his bedroom? Wearing his Stanford T-shirt?

She placed the hot mug in his hands, then curled her legs up onto the bed.

Bare legs. Bare to the thigh. Bare beyond the thigh.

"You going to drink that, or is there something else you'd like better?"

He took a long, deep swallow of coffee. The liquid scalded his tongue and throat, but he didn't flinch.

Ariana Karas was sitting half-naked in his bed, her dark eyes and soft mouth plush with the warmth of a woman well loved, and he had absolutely no idea why.

"Thanks," he said after his throat cooled.

"Right back at you." She scooted off the bed and shuffled toward the drapes, testing the thick folds for the opening. "You might want to turn away from the light, but I have some things on the balcony I need before I can leave."

"Leave?"

She let out a soft, "Aha!" when she found the opening, twisting her body through so that the sunlight didn't flash his sensitive eyes. He took another sip of coffee—prepared just the way he liked it with one sugar and a heavy dose of cream—and wondered what in the hell she'd left outside. He didn't remember going outside. Hell, he didn't remember coming home.

He squeezed his eyes shut. A few vague images answered his desperate summons, but most placed him at Athens by the Bay. A match. He remembered something about…lighting a fire?

When Ariana reentered wearing a pair of unzipped and unbuttoned black jeans beneath his T-shirt, his hold on the recovered memories slipped away. A bra and panties, pink and satiny, dangled from her hand alongside a long-sleeved turtleneck.

"Ariana?"

She looked up at him expectantly and he realized he hadn't really said her name for any other reason than to reassure himself that she really was in his room.

"Max?"

The staring game that followed lasted several seconds. Max watched the expression on Ariana's amazing face progress from boldly flirtatious to slightly shocked.

"You don't remember last night, do you?"

He'd never heard a question he wanted to answer less. "Not yet," he admitted, hoping that once the two-ton fog lifted from his brain, maybe after more coffee and a hot shower, he'd regain whatever he'd lost.

And from the look in her eyes, he'd lost a great deal.

She shook her head. "I didn't think...you seemed all right by the time we..." She huffed in frustration, but until she completed a sentence with information he could use, Max was sure he had the market on confusion.

"Memory loss is a side effect," she finished.

"Side effect of...?"

Ariana folded her undergarments into the turtleneck and rolled them into a ball she twisted tight between her hands. She shuffled uncomfortably for a moment, then strode boldly forward and sat on the bed again, this time at a greater distance than before and without the fluid grace and sensuality she'd shown him when he'd first awakened. She was all business.

"You were at my restaurant last night for dinner and, afterward, you and Charlie came in to the bar for drinks. Do you remember any of that?"

Max closed his eyes. Images warred with the pounding pressure squeezing his skull. He remembered a crowd cheering. A flaming swirl of colors captured in a tall glass. Ariana touching her finger to her luscious, moist mouth.

"Vaguely," he said. He downed another big swallow of coffee. He'd known Ariana for two years, since he moved into his Russian Hill home and started jogging to the office, stopping at her restaurant in the mornings for coffee and in the afternoons for a beer. Never in that time had she ever, ever been cold, but her natural friendliness and warmth had never extended into flirting or come-ons.

Yet here she was, wearing his shirt and sitting on his mattress after gathering her underwear from the balcony outside his bedroom.

"I didn't make it to the restaurant until just before closing," she explained. "But sometime during the evening, someone added something to your drink."

"A drug?"

She shrugged. "I suspect. Something that made it hard for you to focus, loosened your inhibitions and, obviously, affected your memory."

There was a great deal of information to process in what she'd said, but the phrase "loosened your inhibitions" begged to be dealt with first.

Max arched an eyebrow in amusement. "I didn't know I had any inhibitions that needed loosening."

Ariana pressed her lips together, fighting a smile and losing horribly. "Maybe inhibitions isn't the right word," she amended, pretending to scratch her nose when she was really trying to hide her grin.

He sat up straighter and finished the coffee. His memory was still a fuzzy blur, but the jackhammer in his head seemed to have moved a few yards down the block. Her battle with laughter fueled his ire enough to jolt him with energy.

"Then what is the right word?"

She stood up and stepped toward the door. "I think goodbye would work. Someone was probably just playing a joke on you. A harmless one, really, since you're obviously fine and your memory will come back. Little by little, I'll bet."

"You brought me home?"

She inched toward the door, hooking her hand on the knob. "Seemed like the right thing to do at the time. I wanted to make sure you were okay. Whatever happened, happened in my restaurant, but I didn't have anything to do with it and I'm certain none of my employees did either."

Max rubbed his chin, wincing at the thick growth itching his skin. He leaned across the bed and tugged his alarm clock, which was dangling over the bed-stand by the cord.

Eleven forty-five.

Eleven forty-five! He *never* slept that late, even on a Saturday.

That thought gave him pause.

"Today is Saturday, right?" he asked.

She nodded.

Panic clutched his heart as his gaze drifted back to the glowing blue numbers on his alarm clock.

"Saturday the twenty-sixth?"

"Uh-huh."

"Holy…" He followed the oath with an expletive that made Ariana jump even before he vaulted out of the bed and scrambled down the stairs to the kitchen. He paused long enough to get his bearings, then shot toward the two-by-two bulletin board tucked into a

corner of his custom-made cabinets. There, beside the
note from his housekeeper with the dates of her vacation and a neatly penned grocery list that he was
supposed to fax to his delivery service, was an em-
bossed square of thick ivory parchment with elegant
gold lettering. He snatched the invitation off the
board.

*Saturday, the twenty-sixth day of May, the year of
our Lord...*

He read back until he found the time.

Twelve noon.

And to make sure he punished himself, he jumped
to the third line from the top.

*...the marriage of their daughter, Madelyn Jose-
phine Burrows, to Mr. Maxwell Forrester.*

He swore again, suddenly realizing that he was
standing near the window wearing nothing but a
stricken expression. Ariana stared from the doorway,
undoubtedly wondering if he'd lost his mind.

"Are you okay?" she asked for the second time
this morning. Or was it the third?

"I'm late for the wedding."

She echoed his curse. "Charlie's going to kill me.
You're his best man!" She rushed to him and grabbed
the invitation. "What time is it at?"

But she obviously didn't find the noon notation
first. Her eyes enlarged into big black saucers. Her
jaw dropped with an audible gasp. Slowly, those ebony saucers hovered upward to focus on him.

"*You're* getting married today? Charlie told me *he*
was the groom!"

Max glanced down at his bare stomach, somewhat
surprised that the punched-in-the-gut sensation came
from his own guilt rather than her fist to his midsec-

tion. He sure deserved it. He was getting married today and, loveless marriage or not, he'd just cheated
on his fiancée. The fact that Maddie would understand
wasn't the point. Max prefaced his answer with a
string of self-deprecating curses. Some for Maddie,
whom he'd betrayed. And some for Ariana, who
didn't deserve to be used and deceived.

"Charlie lied. But I shouldn't have…we shouldn't…"
It was his turn to leave a phrase unfinished. He
shouldn't have what? Allowed someone to slip something in his drink? Agreed to a marriage of convenience? Denied the desire he'd had for Ariana over
the past two years simply because a woman like her
would undeniably complicate his life?

Ariana looked at the invitation again, then back at
Max, then back at the invitation. "I knew Charlie was
lying about something, but never about this!" She
swallowed hard, then closed her eyes and took a deep
breath. "Get dressed. You have fifteen minutes. I'll
find your car keys."

ARIANA FOUND THE KEYS in the ignition of a current-
model Porsche convertible parked in a pristine garage.
With no idea how to disengage the security alarm
blinking red and ominous on the garage door, she
plopped into the driver's seat. It had been a while
since she'd been behind the wheel of a car. Studying
the instrumentation, she forced herself to focus on
reacquainting herself with the process, when all she
really wanted to do was scream bloody murder.

She'd spent the night with the groom! Not the best
man. The groom! Why had Charlie lied to her? She
couldn't really be mad at Max. She had been convinced last night and still was today that his condition

had not been faked—though she had believed that he was clear and fully aware of his actions once he'd joined her on the balcony. But *she* should have been thinking clearly all night. She had made the choice to go through with the seduction in the fog…then in the bedroom—oh, and the shower. She couldn't forget the shower.

Oh, God! Only her second lover in her entire lifetime and she'd descended from virtual virgin to certified slut in one night? She'd made love with a man on the eve of his wedding to someone else. The fact that she didn't know he was getting married was no excuse, right? That was Charlie's fault. When she got her hands on that liar, she was going to make him pay.

Max slammed into the garage, denying her time to pile on more thoughts of revenge. Right now, all she could do was help him set things right. Unshaven and uncombed, but at least now dressed in pants and a shirt, a bow tie and tuxedo jacket clutched in his left hand, Max punched in the security code and activated the garage opener. Ariana turned the key on the ignition as he yanked open the passenger door and folded himself inside. Whoever had ridden with him last had not been tall.

Probably the bride, "Madelyn Josephine Burrows." Damn her.

"Do you know where St. Armand's Church is?" he asked.

"Unless it's Greek Orthodox, nope."

Max took a deep breath and closed his eyes. "Take a right out the driveway. And step on it." He flipped the tie around his neck and dropped the sun visor to use the vanity mirror.

"Max, about last night..." she said, revving the engine. Now, if she only knew what to say next.

Max stopped fiddling with his tie and laid his hand over hers. "Ari, do what I did. For now, just forget last night."

She pursed her lips as she tested the give-and-take of the clutch. "Easy for you to say. You had pharmaceutical help."

He squeezed her knuckles, then covered her hand completely, enveloping her fingers in his warmth. Ariana focused on the shape and size of his hand, instantaneously remembering the gentle skill that hand had practiced on every inch of her body. Her palms grew slick and her stomach turned.

She'd made love, freely and wildly, with a man who would, as soon as she shoved the car into drive and found the church, marry someone else.

She shook his hand away and manipulated the stick shift into first gear. "I'll be fine. You finish dressing and do the navigating thing. We have a wedding to get to."

THE PARKING LOT was virtually empty. Ari leaned over and checked the clock on the dashboard. It was only quarter past noon. Surely they'd wait fifteen minutes.

Ariana pulled into a space beside the single occupant of the lot, a shiny Honda Accord with several religious stickers on the bumper. "You sure this is the right place?"

Max dug into his pocket for the invitation.

"St. Armand's," he read, then gestured to the marble sign below the statue in the courtyard. "This is where we were last night for the rehearsal."

Ariana hadn't intended to get out of the car. She'd wanted to stop at a restaurant two blocks away and let Max drive the rest of the way alone while she called her uncle to pick her up. She didn't want anyone getting the wrong impression—which, technically, was the right impression if they thought Max had arrived at his wedding with the woman he'd picked up at a bar and slept with the night before his marriage.

But Max, still struggling with his damn tie while she ruined his clutch, begged her to stay with him until they'd reached the church, though he hadn't said why, not even when she'd asked.

"Is there another parking lot?" she ventured, trying to work a reasonable explanation out of a puzzling situation.

"Not that I know of. This is the pastor's car," he said, clicking open his door. "Come on."

Turning off the ignition, she exited the car and tossed him the keys. "Come on? I'm not going anywhere near that church! I have a particularly strong aversion to lightning smiting me dead."

His frown was incorrigible, and so damn cute. "You're a friend getting me to my wedding when I was too hungover to drive. No one is going to assume anything else. Not from Maxwell Forrester. Trust me on that."

His self-deprecating tone intrigued her. "What are you, some kind of Goody Two-shoes?"

He shrugged into his jacket, engaged the car alarm and pocketed the keys. "Something like that," he answered, motioning her to follow when he started up the stone walkway.

Ariana dug her hands into her pockets beneath the

hem of her untucked turtleneck. Her curiosity was on overdrive. She simply didn't know what she wanted to learn more—where all the guests were or what this Madelyn Josephine Burrows looked like.

She stepped around the car and skipped up onto the sidewalk, drawing the brim of her lucky cap slightly downward while she matched her steps to Max's. "What the hell? Maybe I can find a confessional while I'm here."

Max didn't answer and judging by the way he scanned the church for anyone, much less someone familiar, she realized he had much more on his mind than the eternal damnation of her soul. The one time, *the one time*, she decided to throw caution to the wind and have a glorious adventure, she'd wrecked a man's future.

They entered the church through a side door and found the pastor, dressed casually in black pants and a short-sleeved white shirt, fiddling with the position of a glorious bouquet of satiny white tulips in front of the altar.

"Reverend?" Max asked quietly, stopping at the bottom step of the dais.

"Mr. Forrester? What on earth are you doing here?"

Max stared at the man for a long minute, then glanced over his shoulder for Ariana's help. She had paused halfway down the aisle behind him, her expression purposefully blank. She had no more idea than he did about what the heck was going on.

"What am I doing here? Well, I thought I was getting married."

The reverend, who was barely pushing forty and had streaks of gray at his temples and a spry, slender physique, placed his hands on his hips and gave Max a half scolding, half amused smile. "Well, so did I until Mrs. Burrows called this morning to tell me that you and Miss Madelyn had eloped in the dead of night."

The cleric squinted at Ari, who smiled and gave him a little wave. "You're not Miss Madelyn."

Ariana smiled. No, she wasn't. But she wasn't saying a word.

"She's a friend. She drove me here." The explanation rushed out before he stopped and nearly shouted, "Eloped?"

"I take it Mrs. Burrows wasn't telling the whole truth?"

"Eloped?" he repeated.

Max backed up until his legs hit a chair festooned with tulle and bows and he plopped into it. Ari took a step forward, then stopped. This was none of her business. She shouldn't be here. But, good Lord, did Max just get left at the altar?

Why would any woman leave this man at the altar? Ariana slapped her hand over her mouth to contain a gasp. She and Max had made love outside! What if someone saw? What if Madelyn saw? *Oh, God.* What if Max's poor innocent bride had stumbled on to them sometime during the night or morning and, heartbroken, had her mother lie to the priest and all the guests? Ari slid into a pew and buried her face in her hands. She was going to hell for sure.

The pastor's voice carried across the empty church. "I take it Mrs. Burrow's explanation for the cancellation of the wedding wasn't true."

Ariana looked up in time to see Max shake his head. "If Madelyn eloped, it wasn't with me."

The pastor stepped down and sat beside Max, laying his hand across his shoulder. "Did the two of you have a fight?"

"I haven't spoken with Maddie since the rehearsal dinner. She left before I settled the bill."

The pastor glanced over his shoulder, his eyes sweeping over Ariana quickly, but with clear suspicion in his gaze. "And you haven't done anything that might have prompted Miss Madelyn's change of heart?"

What? Did she have the word *homewrecker* tattooed on her forehead? Ariana stood, pursing her lips. Dammit, she didn't know Max was getting married! She'd been deliberately deceived by Charlie Burrows. If anyone was going to pay, it was going to be him, and Ariana wasn't going to depend on divine intervention for that retribution.

Charlie had lied to her about who was the groom. Then the bride's mother lied to the priest about Max eloping. Why was this family acting so despicably? Was Charlie really Max's friend? For all she knew, he could have been the one to doctor Max's drink. But why?

Max stood, holding up his hand to stall Ariana from bolting, which she fully planned to do. "I need to find Madelyn."

The pastor nodded, his expression grave. "A wise course of action. Let me know if you need my assistance."

The men shook hands and before Ariana knew it, she and Max were marching back to his car, their footsteps tapping loud on the stones—in time, in sync, as if the rhythm of their bodies were composed by the same master musician.

Just like last night.

"Max," Ariana spoke when they reached the car, pausing as he clicked off the alarm and opened the passenger door for her.

"I'm okay to drive," he assured her. "I *need* to drive."

She shook her head. That wasn't what she was going to say. "You can drop me off at the corner," she answered. "I'll get a ride home."

"No way. Didn't you say that Charlie told you *he* was the one getting married?"

Nodding, she watched with wonder as the rage built in his eyes, turning them from warm sea green to cold pinpoints of emerald fire. "We planned the rehearsal dinner for weeks," she told him. "He kept encouraging me to flirt with you, talking you up and saying how perfect…"

Her voice trailed off. She sounded like an idiot, trying to justify her own stupidity and blind lust. She hated being duped, the pawn in some grand design of someone else's making.

"Get in, Ariana. We've both been screwed, and—"

She didn't mean to laugh, but couldn't help herself.

He touched her arm then, jolting the humor out of her with a shock of awareness that had no right to exist between them but did.

"Bad word choice. I'm sorry."

"I'm the one who should apologize. I just want you to know I don't ever, *ever* sleep with men I hardly know. Last night was…never mind. You don't remember and maybe it's better that you don't. I should leave well enough alone."

His grin was halfhearted, and she thought—hoped—

she saw regret in his eyes. "This is 'well enough'? I just got jilted."

"Maybe someone saw us together."

That erased the half smile from his mouth.

"Maybe. But we won't know until we ask some questions. Charlie owes *both* of us an explanation." He stepped back and opened the car door farther. "I'll try to get one out of him before I wring his neck."

Ariana couldn't disagree. She wanted to find Charlie as soon as possible and she had no way of knowing how to do that without Max. She also wanted to wring Charlie's neck first, but she'd argue for that right after they found him.

"Aren't you going to call Madelyn?" she asked, sliding into the car.

Max didn't answer. He slammed her door shut and walked around to the driver's side, got in, turned the key and backed up with perfect grace. He'd undoubtedly left all vestiges of his hangover in the church vestibule.

"Max, why don't you let me deal with Charlie and you go see Madelyn?"

He shook his head as he maneuvered out of the parking lot. "Maddie can wait until I find out the details."

Men! He'd been duped and drugged, and he probably suspected Charlie had something to do with that. She couldn't blame him. Charlie was suspect number one in her eyes, too. But she was perfectly capable of torturing the truth out of Charlie on her own. Max had something more important to do.

"Max, you need to see Maddie. She could be crying her eyes out because the man she loves cheated on her the night before their wedding. She's probably humiliated!''

At the stoplight, he twisted into his seat belt then motioned for Ariana to do the same. Cool and calm didn't begin to describe the precision of his movements, the controlled expression on his face. So this was how a man made millions, Ariana decided. Little by little, Max had reined in his emotions, tucking them away so she could see nothing but concentration on his face.

"I'll take care of Maddie. I promised to do that. I don't break promises."

Ariana sat back into the seat, silenced. He'd pledged last night to pleasure her beyond her wildest fantasies, to touch her precisely where she wanted to be touched, and show her a few places she hadn't known would lead her to complete ecstasy. A thrumming heat suffused her veins as each caress, each kiss, replayed in her mind. Their interlude had been about abandon, exploration, unhindered freedom. She hadn't imagined or intended that they'd hurt anyone in the process.

She'd learned things about herself, about her body, about her needs, that she'd treasure forever. How many women would be so lucky? She knew then that if Max said he'd take care of Maddie, she would believe him.

Max Forrester was most definitely a man of his word.

6

"CHARLIE, OPEN THIS DAMN DOOR!"

Max pounded and jabbed the doorbell until he was certain that if anyone was inside Charlie and Sheri's North Beach walk-up, they were either dead or scared shitless to answer. He growled, knowing his best friend, conniving son of a bitch that he was, would never cower or hide. He'd face the music, no matter how loud or how ugly. It was one of the reasons he loved Charlie, bastard that he was.

"I don't think anyone's home, Max."

Ariana leaned on the front end of his Porsche, looking remarkably like one of those calendar models his mechanic had all over his shop. Except that her clothes covered nearly every inch of her skin, from her jaunty cap to her long-sleeved shirt, snug jeans and boots. He jabbed his fingers through his hair before he attacked the door again. To add to his frustration, he had very little trouble imagining her in nothing but those pink satin underthings she'd dangled from her fingers earlier. Too little trouble. He rightfully felt like a lying, cheating jerk, and women like Ariana Karas, and Maddie, deserved a hell of a lot better.

Giving up at the door, he jogged to the car, parked halfway on the curb and grabbed his Daytimer from the back seat. Ripping out a page, he carved a note with his felt-tip pen, then flashed it at Ariana so she could see he was serious.

Call me or you're fired. Max.

"What? No death threat?" she asked.

"Charlie just got married a few months ago. Sheri has expensive tastes. Threatening his life won't be nearly as effective as promising to cut off his income."

"Funny," Ari quipped. "I was planning on cutting off something else that Charlie's wife values."

Max raised an eyebrow, but Ariana didn't crack a smile or give him any indication that she wasn't dead serious.

Note to self: Don't piss this woman off.

Max pinned the paper beneath the door knocker and then slid back into the car as Ari did the same. He started the engine and pulled onto Greenwich Street before he realized he didn't know where to go next.

"If you can't find Charlie, shouldn't you call Madelyn?"

Ariana's concern for Maddie made Max feel even worse, not that he didn't care about Maddie himself. Nothing could be further from the truth. But he did know without a doubt that Maddie was not and never had been in love with him. No matter what happened to cause her to call off the wedding, Maddie wasn't experiencing the level of betrayal Ariana undoubtedly imagined.

They were just friends working out a mutually beneficial deal. Weren't they? All of a sudden, Max wasn't so sure. He had, technically, cheated. The act alone, drug-induced or not, denoted a lack of loyalty that tasted bitter in his mouth. Maddie didn't deserve such treachery.

And Ariana? What could she possibly be thinking, knowing she'd been lied to and deceived? For the moment, she focused on Maddie's feelings, but sooner or later she'd have her own to deal with, just as he'd have his. However, her apparent concern over his fiancée rather than herself only proved yet again that Ariana Karas was too good for the likes of him.

"It really bothers you that she might have gotten hurt, doesn't it?"

"*Might have gotten hurt?* She called off her wedding, Max. She made up an elaborate story about you eloping. Why else would she do that unless she saw us together last night? We weren't exactly practicing the depth of discretion."

He remained silent, but made a choice. He'd find Maddie soon enough and explain everything until she understood and forgave him. He'd take care of her, just as he'd promised. But right now he couldn't fight the urge to sustain whatever connection he'd formed with Ariana.

He'd dreamed about her for so long, cast her in countless forbidden fantasies. He couldn't waste this chance to fix what had gone so horribly wrong. The reverberation in her voice told him she blamed herself for last night's liaison.

If only she knew how he'd spent quite a few nights staring from his empty bed out to the view he'd paid way too much money for, wishing he could share the skyline with someone as intrinsically drawn to the hypnotic vista as he was.

He'd shown the view to Maddie once—and not from the vantage of the bed—but when she looked out onto any part of San Francisco, all she saw were the sights that needed to be changed. The beaches suffering corrosion. The neighborhoods overrun with liquor stores and strip clubs. The houses being renovated with no respect for the architect's original intentions or the character of the building or street.

He loved Maddie, in the way good friends should, but she wasn't the woman for him any more than he was the man for her. He'd never once fantasized about stripping her bare on a clear, cool night, then making love to her outside, with the stars and the city as witnesses to their passion.

But he'd imagined it with Ariana Karas, more times than he cared to count.

"I'll take you home first and then I'll call Maddie. I'm sure she's fine."

"Shouldn't you go *find* Maddie?"

Max shook his head, then shrugged. Honestly, he didn't know what to do. His anger subsided long enough for him to realize that his head was pounding like a bass drum. As much as he'd like to think he knew Maddie better than anyone, he couldn't be certain about how she would react if she had somehow stumbled on to him and Ariana last night. They'd never pretended to love one another *that* way. They hadn't even talked about how they'd handle sex during their marriage.

Up until last night, he hadn't put much value or importance on sex. His priority had been achieving his business goals and establishing himself as an independent, successful powerbroker in the world of San Francisco real estate. And so far as he knew, Maddie felt the same way.

But judging by the stricken expression shadowing

Ariana's face, he needed to explain his arrangement with Maddie before she traded her tight turtleneck for a hair shirt.

"Look, Ari, I know you feel guilty about Madelyn. But we didn't have that kind of relationship."

Ariana glanced at him sideways and puckered her lips while she considered what he meant. Spending his adult years in San Francisco had taught him never to let uncertainties linger. There were too many deviations available in the city, too many possibilities for why he and Maddie's marriage would have been purely platonic. And dammit, he didn't want Ari thinking he swung the other way.

"That didn't sound right," he said.

"No, it didn't. If you've been thinking all these years that you were gay, I hate to be the one to break it to you..."

"I don't think I'm gay," he insisted.

She smacked her lips. "That makes two of us."

Part of him was pleased. Part of him was frustrated beyond frustration that he had no memory of why she'd be so smugly certain.

"Good."

"So..." she sang, obviously wanting—and deserving—more explanation than he'd given her.

"Maddie and I have been friends a long time, since college."

"That's sweet," she injected, clear by her tone that she was only half-sincere. "You marrying a woman you weren't sleeping with and had no intention of sleeping with? That's what you're trying to tell me, right? Why?"

She was too damn smart for her own good. And

for his. "We had a mutually beneficial arrangement planned."

Boy, that sounded cold when he said it out loud.

"You were using each other," she clarified.

"No! I mean, well, not exactly."

"Using is using whether it's friendly or spiteful. She wanted something from you, you wanted something from her, all the cards are laid out on the table and everyone's happy. So why then did she call off the wedding and tell everyone the two of you eloped? Do you think she was seeing someone?"

"Maddie?"

Ariana's expression told him she heard the fury in his outburst. His tone surprised him as well.

He turned north onto Grant Avenue, for no other reason than because he had wanted to feel as if he was going somewhere. Somewhere other than down the road where he learned he'd taken Maddie for granted.

"If Maddie had found someone, she would have told me. I've encouraged her for years to look for someone who would love her, but she wasn't interested in having her heart broken."

Ariana nodded silently, as if she commiserated with Maddie on a personal level he didn't want to contemplate. He didn't want to think about some man hurting Ariana any more than he wanted to think about hurting Maddie. The idea introduced a hint of rage more potentially harmful than the murderous intentions he planned to wreak on Charlie whenever he got his hands on him.

Of course, at the moment, the man who could potentially hurt Ariana most of all was him, unless he did something to avert the inevitable. Right here. Right now.

"If Maddie did see us together and did call off the wedding," he said, hoping to ease Ariana's persistent guilt, "I'm pretty sure she'd do it because she thought it would make me happy, not because she felt betrayed or angry."

"Pretty sure isn't the same as certain."

"No, it's not. But I'll find out." Without thinking, he reached across and laid his hand over hers. "Trust me."

A grin bloomed, despite her apparent effort to tamp it down. "I've already done that."

"Any regrets?"

She turned her hand over so her palm nestled with his.

"Just that you don't remember."

"There's no way in hell you regret that more than I do."

They sat silently at a traffic light, hand in hand, warmth to warmth. In the close quarters of his compact car, her scent, citrusy and fresh like a beach breeze, drifted in the air-conditioned space, teasing him, taunting him. Max shut his eyes against the bright sun, willing his brain to conjure a single clear image from the night before. Something wonderful. Something sweet. Something he could hold on to during the mess he was about to endure with Maddie, his parents, her parents and the entire social elite of San Francisco.

He got nothing but a dusky fog.

When he turned left at Bay Street, Ariana realized he was wandering and gave him directions to double back to her apartment in Chinatown. He released her hand to shift the gears and she busied herself with looking over the instrumentation of the car, asking him about the features as if she was honestly interested.

"Is this a car phone?" She pointed to the console.

"Yes. It's hands-free, for safety. There's a headset hidden in this panel if I need privacy."

"What's this blinking red light?"

Max glanced away from the road long enough to catch a ruby glimmer in the corner of his eye.

"A message."

He turned at Mason Street, glad when a cable car stopped in front of him so he could take a closer look.

"But no one calls me on this number. No one except..." He jabbed the playback button and tensed as the mechanical voice announced he had one message—from Maddie.

"Do you want the headset?" Ariana asked.

Before he could reply, Madelyn's cultured voice, soft and sad, echoed over the clanging of the cable car and the rumble of his engine. "Hi, Max. It's Maddie. I feel like such a coward. I should be telling you goodbye in person, but I've got to get away while I can. I'm sorry if I've embarrassed you, if I've ruined everything. But I've got to do this. I'll call you once I figure out where I'm going. Don't worry. For once, I'm going to be okay on my own. You might want to lay low for a couple of days, pretend we really are in Hawaii. I love you."

Max pulled over onto the first driveway he saw and worked the buttons until the message replayed. Ariana didn't say a word, but stared at him with confused eyes.

"I don't understand what she means," he admitted. "Why is she apologizing to me?"

"Play it again."

He did. The third time was not the charm. He still had no idea what Maddie was talking about, but he did catch the automatic announcement of when the call was received—just before midnight the evening before.

"What time did we leave the restaurant?" he asked.

"Just before one o'clock, clearly after she called."

They both sighed in relief, but Ariana couldn't shake the feeling that something more was wrong with Madelyn. She didn't know the woman—she shouldn't care. But she did.

"She may not have known anything about us when she made this call," Ariana said, "but something is going on with her. How does she sound to you?"

Max replayed the message, this time listening for the emotions in Maddie's voice. She was slightly nervous, but clear. A sound of intense determination deepened her tone, despite her apologetic words.

"She sounds like a woman with a plan, which for Maddie is somewhat normal."

"She sounded a little scared to me," Ariana added.

Max nodded. He did hear anxiety in Maddie's tone, but nothing that got his hackles up or engaged his protective instincts. He and Maddie had known each other for so long, he felt confident he'd know when and if to be worried.

And he wasn't worried. Maddie may have finally come to her senses and realized that their marriage would have been a huge mistake for her. He'd tried to tell her that she shouldn't work so hard at living up to the expectations of others at the expense of her own wants and needs, but it was an empty argument coming from him. Wasn't he guilty of the same crime? Maddie needed time and space and, like the clever minx she was, she'd probably cooked up the elopement ruse to cover her escape.

He couldn't help but grin. When push came to shove, she'd always been the more courageous of the two of them. Looked as if he needed to take a lesson from his best bud once again.

"She sounds a little scared, but a whole lot more determined." He shifted the car back onto the main road, nodding quietly as they progressed, proud of Madelyn for making a stand, even in this roundabout way. "I think Maddie has gone off to find herself and used the elopement as a smoke screen."

Ariana sat back in the leather bucket seat and chewed her bottom lip as she processed all the information he'd given her, asking questions at intermittent moments between giving directions to her home, clarifying her understanding and filling in the gaps.

"So, Maddie was marrying you because…"

"She was tired of the pressure from her parents to get married. And the women she worked with in her building-restoration efforts were older, very conservative—they had an elemental distrust of a female over twenty-one who wasn't properly wed to a man of power and prestige."

"And now you think she ran away to get her priorities straight and told everyone the two of you eloped?"

He shrugged. "Well, either Maddie cooked that one up or her parents did when they realized she was AWOL. They wouldn't stand for something so humiliating as a runaway daughter, even if she is nearly thirty years old.''

''And you don't think you should go look for her? Make certain she's okay?''

He shook his head. ''Definitely not. Maddie knows exactly how to contact me if she needs to.''

Ariana accepted his claim with a nod. ''Pull into that alley. You can park behind the shop. There aren't any deliveries on Saturday.''

Max concentrated as he made the sharp right turn into a narrow alley between the blocks of Pacific and Powell. Driving in wasn't so hard, but the thought of them opening the doors to get out caused the imaginary sound of metal scraping brick to echo in his head. Still, what was a little scratched paint when he had the chance to see where Ariana Karas lived?

''Is the car safe here?'' he asked, eyeing the deserted alley with the skeptical glare of a man who rarely ventured into Chinatown except to take some out-of-town client for dim sum.

''Well, there's always an off chance that Mr. Ping's rooster will take a liking to your convertible top.''

''Mr. Ping's rooster lives in the alley?''

''No, the rooster lives in his guest bathroom, but he comes out here for fresh air.''

''Are you teasing me?''

She winked before she flipped open the door with just enough speed to make him wince and enough alacrity not to scrape the door on the wall. ''If you had any memory of last night, you'd know I'm not a tease.''

Grabbing her backpack from the tiny space behind her seat, she shut the door with due care and slipped around to his side.

"You coming in?" she asked through the glass, her thumb hooked toward the dingy metal door neatly hand-painted with "Madame Li's Herb Shop. Deliveries here," first in Chinese, then in English.

He took the key out of the ignition and opened his door just wide enough to bend out of the car.

"I'm invited?"

"Well, let's see." She slung the backpack over one shoulder, where it promptly hit the wall, then she ticked off her reasons on her fingers. "Your fiancée just jilted you for parts unknown so she could go find herself. She or her family has told everyone that's important to you that you've eloped. I assume you've already arranged for a week off from work and I doubt anyone would dare to contact a newlywed on his honeymoon. And since the only person either you or I feel compelled to contact is probably going to make himself scarce today, can you think of anything else you need to do? Other than come upstairs with me?"

Her smile was reserved, but no less filled with possibilities.

"So you're saying I should come with you because I have nothing else to do?"

She frowned, just as he'd expected, just as he'd hoped. He didn't remember anything solid from last night's encounter, but if he was going to start over, nurturing this connection between them—at least for the week she had pointed out he now had free and clear—he wouldn't let her think she was anything but his first choice.

Because even before they'd made love, she had been his first choice. His only choice.

"Ouch," she said. "That's not what I meant at all."

He slammed the car door shut and clicked on the alarm. Two quick beeps told him the automobile was shielded from thieves, though he wasn't entirely sure about Chinese roosters.

"I didn't think it was. That's why I pointed it out."

She smiled and nodded, obviously appreciating his pragmatic reasoning. "So, if you're not coming up because you have nothing else to do, why are you?" she asked.

He edged around the side mirror, stepping into the inches separating Ariana from the hood of his car. She straightened against the wall, her backpack further padding them close. With his tuxedo jacket and tie tossed unceremoniously in the trunk and his shirt unbuttoned, he could feel her breasts mold softly—bralessly—against his chest. The effect was an instantaneous hardening of his sex.

"Think Madame Li had something to alleviate my headache?" Seconds ticked by before she looked up at him, then down at his obvious erection, then back up with a slanted glance that was half saucy bravado and half blatant interest.

"If she doesn't, I think I may have something to ease your discomfort."

MADAME LIN LI WAS a tall woman, statuesque in every sense of the word. Her great-great-grandmother had been the concubine of a Norwegian prince, so her nearly six-foot height and pale blue eyes were attributed to his genetic influence. But otherwise, she was Chinese in every sense of the word. Proud of her ancient heritage, Madame Li wore her sleek, embroidered satin dress with all the beauty of an Oriental princess, her jet-black hair twisted and secured with enamel chopsticks festooned with tiny red ribbons.

Her shrewd eyes and keen business sense, however, were decidedly American. The minute Ariana and Max passed from the alley into her kitchen, the private room she used to brew her specialty teas for her customers, her pencil-thin eyebrows shot up over wide eyes.

Ariana gave her a respectful bow. "Good morning, Madame Li. This is Maxwell Forrester. He's a friend."

Madame Li gracefully lifted a copper teakettle from her gas-burning stove and doused the blue flame. She nodded at Max while she poured the hot water into a porcelain pot etched with fine blue Chinese symbols.

"A new friend, Mr. Forrester? I've never heard Ariana speak of you."

He bowed respectfully, all the while stretching his hands in his pockets so Mrs. Li didn't see the most pressing reason for his interest in her boarder.

"We've known each other for a few years."

She hummed her suppositions, but kept her obvious skepticism to herself.

"I was hoping you could brew a tea for Max," Ariana said. "He has a terrible headache. Someone put something into his drink at the restaurant last night."

"On purpose?" Mrs. Li asked.

Max shook his head, but Ariana shrugged. She knew he didn't believe the drug was put in his drink accidentally. He suspected Charlie just as much as she did. Apparently, he didn't want to discuss the matter with a stranger. She couldn't blame him. Ariana had invited Max into her home, something she hadn't done for any other man since she'd been married. She was taking another chance based on the two things they had in common: a betrayal by Charlie Burrows and a rather hot attraction. They absolutely had to deal with the first one. With regards to the second, well, that remained to be seen.

Ariana knew what she wanted, but whether or not grabbing the brass ring for a second time was prudent, she wasn't entirely sure. But she sure as heck wouldn't know the answer if she just sent Max on his merry way, now, would she?

"What happened, exactly?" Mrs. Li asked.

Ariana looked askance and Max pressed his lips together.

The Asian matron chuckled. "Okay, forget I said 'exactly.' Just give me a list of your symptoms, Mr. Forrester."

"I was drowsy and disoriented at first, then..."

Ariana filled in the blanks in the most delicate way she could. "He was very...relaxed."

Madame Li listened as she placed several teacups and saucers on a tray beside the brewing pot. "And this morning?"

Max shook his head, as if to clear the cobwebs. "I can't remember much, if anything, about last night. And there's the headache."

Mrs. Li lifted the tray and placed it on an ornate, carved teacart without jangling one cup. "I have four ladies waiting for tea, but I'll mix something up and bring it to you."

"I can come down," Ariana insisted. She admired Mrs. Li a great deal and already felt as if she was taking advantage of her hospitality by bringing Max in through her back door, like a teenager trying to sneak a boyfriend into her bedroom. Not that Ariana knew about that. But Madame Li had been her land-lady for going on eight years, renting first to Rick and then subbing the lease to Ariana after he took off. If Ariana didn't spend so much time at the restaurant and so little time at home, they might have developed a mother-daughter relationship.

As it was, they were friends. Friends who shared a few secrets—including Ariana's reluctance to let a man into her life again. And yet, here she was, ush-ering one upstairs into her room.

Mrs. Li shooed Ariana and Max toward the back stairs. "You have other matters to tend to. I'll bring the tea. Now, out of my kitchen."

Ariana thanked Mrs. Li again and led Max by the hand behind the silk curtain that led to a narrow stair-well. They climbed two flights, emerging on the third floor just outside her apartment. She fished her key out of the front pocket of her backpack, and opened the door.

Her window sheers cast a glow like fire into the hall. She saw Max's eyes narrow as he peered around her. He'd see nothing but scarlet until he came in—even after, for that matter.

"I've done some rather interesting decorating," she said by way of enticement. "Care to see?"

She disappeared into the yards of red silk she'd draped across the archway leading into her rooms. She dropped the backpack atop her black enamel trea-sure chest and tossed her hat onto the head of a five-foot-long ceramic dragon.

Walking into her apartment always made her feel as if she'd entered a different world—a luxurious, exotic world with ancient secrets and erotic promise. And when the door shut behind Max, she realized her world wasn't just bolts of secondhand fabric and rescued treasures from Madame Li's attic anymore.

Max's presence made her home the stuff of fantasies. And if Ariana knew one thing about Max, she knew he was a man who could make all sorts of fantasies come true.

7

"SO? WHAT DO YOU THINK?"

In all his fantasies about Ariana Karas, never once had he imagined what sort of place she lived in. If he had, he most definitely wouldn't have dreamed up this decor. Not that he didn't like it. What man wouldn't like a room that was a cross between a harem den and a Buddhist temple?

"It's very red." Going for the obvious seemed like the smartest move, particularly when his real reaction bordered on obscene. Okay, not obscene, but depraved. No, not that either. Not with Ariana. Memory loss or not, he guessed that making love with her had been nothing short of glorious. In a setting like this, he might not ever want to leave her bed.

Or more factually, he'd never want to leave the endless collection of thick, embroidered throw pillows scattered on her shiny hardwood floors and over the plush carpets.

"I like red," she said with pride. She moved across the room to a black enamel table and lit a thin reed of incense. The scent snaked toward him, teasing his nostrils with a potent spice he couldn't identify. Not as sweet as cinnamon or as pungent as frankincense, the odor brought his senses alive, then seeped into his lungs and relaxed him from the inside out.

"In the morning, this room is very cheery." She

touched a long match to a row of candles and then
opened windows and switched on lamps capped with
paper-thin shades. "In the evenings, it's soothing."

And in the afternoon, it's erotic as hell.

"Make yourself comfortable." She gestured toward the mound of pillows he realized was actually
a couch. "Do you want the phone? I'm going to take
a shower, if you don't mind."

I wouldn't mind taking a shower with you.

"Phone would be good. I'm going to see if Charlie
is hiding out at the office."

She grabbed a portable phone from around a doorway he assumed was an entrance to her kitchen, but
a reluctant pause accompanied her handing it to him.

"What?" he asked.

"Just be careful who you call."

"Why?"

She bit her lower lip, hooking her fingers into her
belt loops again while she rocked on her heels. "You
have a unique opportunity here. Too many phone
calls could ruin it."

God, her eyes were fathomless. Black as the finish
on her furniture, yet as soulful as the ancient accou-
trements she'd placed around her home. Ariana Karas
was a mystery, no less fascinating or arousing as a
foreign land to an explorer. The opportunity she
spoke of wasn't lost on him. She was ever so sweetly
making him an offer he'd be a fool to refuse.

"You mean my chance to have one week of pure
freedom? With no one expecting me to be around?
No one looking for me?"

She grinned and backed away. "A once-in-a-
lifetime opportunity. Just like my week off." Slinging
her backpack over her shoulder, she moved quickly

across the living room to an archway shielded with dark, glossy beads and another layer of silk. "Help yourself to whatever. Look around. I don't have any secrets."

She disappeared through the strands of ebony beads, her departure accompanied by a musical tinkle that reminded him of wind chimes. This small space, no more than three hundred square feet, if his instincts were right, exuded relaxation and escape. She worked long hours at the restaurant; he knew that for a fact. But while he'd hired a decorator to give his home the proper signs of the wealth he slaved for, Ariana had created her very own mystical haven to escape to after the hustle and bustle of her busy workday.

No secrets, huh? Max seriously doubted that. In fact, he knew she had secrets—mainly, the mystery of what really happened between them the night before. He took the phone over to the couch, sighing as the velvet cushions swallowed the aches in his body. He kicked off his shoes and shed his socks, then tucked the polished loafers out of the way.

Stretching his legs, he scanned the room. He had entered a different world. A world where color and texture and scents mixed to create a sensual experience like no other.

An experience he could enjoy for an entire week, if he took a wild chance.

Seven days. No responsibilities. No expectations. Because of the wedding, he'd made certain to close all his major deals last week. He'd signed off on several hundred thousand dollars' worth of real estate transactions that little by little, were making him a very wealthy man. He'd left only one deal open—the big one—the stage of development too early to rush.

It killed him to let the purchase of the old Pier sit for an entire week. Still, he'd talked his partners into putting off any progress until he could give the project his full attention.

Max punched the number to Maddie's parents' house into the phone, calculating his words carefully before the butler answered the call and informed him that the Burrowses were at the reception hall with the rest of the wedding guests, who were celebrating Miss Madelyn's marriage without the bride and groom.

Max grinned. Randolph Burrows wasn't a man to waste money and Barbara Burrows wasn't a woman to miss throwing the social event of the season. Bride and groom? Obviously, unnecessary. He hung up and redialed Randolph's cell phone.

Barbara answered. ''Maxwell? Why are you calling from your honeymoon? Is Madelyn all right?''

That answered his original and most pressing question. The elopement was Maddie's lie, not her family's. Madelyn had crafted a tension-free escape, and laid the groundwork for him to enjoy one of his own.

''Yes, ma'am,'' he answered. ''She's fine.''

She was away from their influence and away from him. Madelyn was more than fine.

''I just wanted to apologize for our…spontaneity.''

''Just as long as you aren't calling about business. I confiscated this phone from Randolph so he'd have a good time.''

Max laughed. ''No, no business. I know you put a great deal of time and effort into the wedding.''

''Not an ounce of which is being wasted, I assure you. You kids have a great time. And don't you worry about that deal you and Randolph have been working on, either. Every one of your investors is here, slurping champagne as if the world will end tomorrow. None of them will be in any condition to think about business for a couple of days at least.''

Max thanked his former would-be mother-in-law and disconnected the call. For an instant, he allowed himself to wonder how Barbara and Randolph would react once they realized that both he and Maddie had lied about their marriage. Of course, if Max managed to make Randolph a millionaire yet again, he was certain he'd be forgiven. Maddie would have to sculpt her own redemption with her parents, if she even wanted their approval anymore. Naturally, he'd help her, but she'd wasted so much of her life seeking the respect of her family, he hoped she'd wait until she was truly ready to make a stand.

Max realized for the first time since he was eight that he had an entire seven days with absolutely no responsibilities, no expectations, nothing. Whether he liked it or not, his big deal was on hold. His office staff had clear instructions to handle all emergencies as if he were dead and even his housekeeper was on vacation. He had nothing to take care of—nothing but a sexy woman showering in the adjoining room...a woman who had the same number of days to escape from everyday life. With him.

The shower stopped running at the same time as a light rap echoed on the door. He set the phone on the cushions and answered the knock. Mrs. Li stood on the other side, greeted him with a slight bow and handed him a laden tray.

''This tea will help you, I think.''

Though probably near fifty years of age, Mrs. Lin Li was an exceptionally attractive woman, partly because of her classic Asian features—almond-shaped eyes, glossy hair and fine skin—and partly because she broke the mold in unexpected ways—her height, light irises and steely carriage. A woman like her commanded respect and Max immediately gave it.

"I appreciate your hospitality, Mrs. Li. I'm sure your tea will work wonders."

"It is not my hospitality you should value. Take care with my boarder, Mr. Forrester. She isn't as worldly as her decor or behavior might indicate."

Mrs. Li wordlessly disappeared down the hall, but her warning was clear. Max promised himself he'd heed it. He set the tray carefully on a low table in front of the couch. Fact was, he didn't know very much about Ariana Karas. About what she knew or didn't know. About what she wanted or didn't want.

But he had an entire week to find out.

ARIANA PROPPED OPEN the bathroom door, spilling a billow of steam into her small, messy bedroom. Damp and aware of Max's presence in the adjoining room, she couldn't tamp down the memory of making love with him in the fog. Seeing and yet not seeing. Using touch to guide touch. Exploring the full breadth of sensual pleasure.

Too bad Max didn't remember a thing.

With a grunt, Ariana twirled her hair into a towel, then dried herself briskly with another. She tried not to think about where Max had run his hands or mouth last night or how wonderful it would be to invite him into her room right now to help her remove the moisture from her skin while he evoked a separate wetness deep inside.

She wondered if he'd accept her invitation until she recalled the hard evidence of his desire that had been more than apparent downstairs when he'd pinned her against the wall.

But even if he didn't remember what happened last night, they had just survived a tense morning-after. They'd done okay, too. He'd made no lame excuses for his questionable judgment with Madelyn, but had given Ari the facts to decipher as she saw fit. And she wanted to believe that Max was incredibly kind, but equally misguided. Marriage, in her experience, was *never* a convenience.

She knew that truth firsthand. Watching her aunt and uncle, whose marriage was even healthier than her parents' thirty-five-year union, had taught her that making a lifetime commitment required more than friendship or mutual goals. Those characteristics helped, but without passion—without love—the union was destined for disaster.

For Max and Madelyn's sake, Ariana was glad they'd learned their lesson before they'd taken their vows. She didn't wish the heartbreak of divorce on anyone. And now that her hot shower seemed to have cleansed away any lingering and unnecessary guilt over her night with Max, Ariana knew she couldn't let this opportunity pass. Max was a free agent. And most important, his interest in her matched the fascination she harbored for him.

Time to grab the fantasy while she could.

Living in Chinatown gave her the advantage of owning one of the most complete collections of silk clothing of any non-Asian woman she knew. She swept through her assortment of silky robes and satin pajamas until she found her favorite: a thick, pink satin robe piped in red and sporting a glorious gold dragon on the back. With care, she laid the robe across her pillows, collected the assortment of discarded clothes and socks and underthings her hectic schedule kept her from gathering throughout the week and tossed them into an overflowing hamper in the corner.

She tidied and straightened wearing nothing but the towel on her head, stopping dead when she heard Max's voice from the other side of the thin curtain. His shoulder or hand must have rustled the beads, because they tinkled in the silence, adding a musical accompaniment to the thrill of hearing him so close while she was so exposed.

"Mrs. Li brought the tea," he announced. She silently inched to the opening, marveling at the subtle change in the atmosphere as she neared him—the way her body reacted instinctively with a pulsing thrum. The man was potent. Potent and dangerous. Just what she needed for a weeklong fling.

"I'll be right there," she whispered, swallowing when the curtain rolled with his movement, brushing inward as he shifted his weight.

They stood silently, mere inches away. One of them had to move away first. But neither did, for a long, torturous minute. Then the ebony glass she'd strung from the archway chimed ever so slightly and the air lost a degree of thickness. She heard Max sigh as he settled back into the cushions of her couch.

She towel-dried her hair, unwilling to waste fifteen minutes with a blow-dryer, combed it out and twisted it up into a loose chignon secured with chopsticks. She applied a dusting of powder and blush to her face, along with a light application of liner and mascara. She used a heavier hand with her lipstick, choosing a brick color that brought out the lush shape of her lips and hinted, however subtly, of the ancient tradition of the Chinese concubine or Japanese geisha.

After spritzing her body with jasmine-scented cologne, she donned the robe and tied the sash with a snug but easily undoable knot. One glance in the mirror reminded her she was an attractive, alluring woman. And attractive, alluring women deserved to live out a fantasy or two, even if only for a week.

And to that end, she unzipped her backpack and retrieved the magazine. The photographs gave her a delicious idea, an inspired plan. And she suspected she wouldn't need much to convince Max to join her.

When she emerged from her bedroom, Max was moving the tray from the credenza to the coffee table. With a shake and rattle, he dropped the tea the last inch.

"Wow."

She twirled around, pausing with her back to him to model the dragon.

"You like?"

Her final half spin swirled the hem of the robe against her bare legs. She watched him swallow thickly and couldn't believe that she'd once considered him standoffish. Uninterested in a woman like her. Untouchable and somewhat remote. The man now wore his desire with the same rumpled charm and sexy innuendo as his half-discarded tuxedo. She forced her triumphant grin into an understated smile, more than willing to take some of the credit for Max's new attitude.

"What's not to like?" he asked.

Snagging her bottom lip in her teeth, she bounced onto the cushions beside the couch with a barely checked energy—a revved mixture of sexual excitement and daring spirit. She slipped the magazine beneath a cushion. First things first.

"Well, let's see. I seduced you on the night before your wedding. That might make a man a little annoyed."

He slung his hands into his pockets and eyed her with an irresistible mix of amusement and disbelief. "I may not remember the details of last night, but I think it's safe to assume we each did a fair and equal amount of seducing."

"Yes," she conceded, "but I was completely sober."

He squatted so they were eye level. "That gives you the advantage of knowing precisely how great we were together. Of course, I'm assuming we were great together or you wouldn't have invited me to your apartment and offered me tea."

She grabbed the edge of the tray and pulled it forward, sliding onto the cushions that had fallen from the couch to the floor beside the table. "That's a fair assumption. Does it bother you that you still can't remember?"

With a tentative touch, he laid his hand over hers while she lined up the cups and saucers.

"Bothered isn't the right word. It's more like torture. You may not know this, but I've been attracted to you for a very long time. Since the first time I saw you."

His hand disappeared beneath the gape in her sleeve, his fingers inching up and down her arm slowly, erotically.

"Really?" she asked with a gulp. "You never flirted or came on to me."

He closed his eyes and grunted in frustration. "No,

I didn't. Just proves once again that when it comes to women, I'm a full-fledged idiot. In hindsight, that drug in my drink may have been the best thing that's ever happened to me.''

She laughed. ''Even with the headache?''

He snorted. ''That's the least of my discomfort, Ariana.''

She pressed her lips together. The silken wet texture of her lipstick, coupled with the image of her smearing the brazen color on his mouth, emboldened her to the point of no return. ''I have an idea that might alleviate your pain.''

From the way his emerald eyes darkened, enhancing the flecks of gold she hadn't noticed until right this moment, she gathered he had a few ideas of his own.

He turned her hand palm up and swirled an erotic shape in the center with his fingertip. ''I was thinking we drink our tea, relax, then go back to my house and wait until tonight. You could reconstruct the evening for me. Kiss by kiss.''

''I like the way you think,'' she admitted, somewhat breathless at the suggestion. But while his idea brimmed with sensual promise, hers bordered on outrageous. Sinfully outrageous.

''But we didn't kiss that much,'' she finished.

''We didn't?''

She shook her head and licked her lips, shocked that her mouth fairly vibrated with anticipation of his kisses.

''See? I obviously wasn't myself. I've spent more hours than I'd care to admit fantasizing about doing nothing more than kiss you.''

The flattery pushed her farther. ''Nothing more?''

she challenged, certain that a grown man like Max would never settle for just kissing. And why should he, when touching and caressing and exploring and mating were so incredible?

"Well, maybe a little more. But only after a lot of kissing."

She nodded and poured the tea into one tiny cup, then the other. The spiced scents of ginger and clove flared her nostrils instantly. This was Madame Li's most potent tea, a mixture of herbs and spices and secrets handed down from generation to generation.

"Smells strong," he commented as she slid the cup over to him. He settled more comfortably into the cushions, folding his legs to his side rather than attempt to squash them beneath the low table.

"Oh, it is. She brewed this tea for me once, a long time ago. It'll clear your head."

He started to lift the cup, but she stopped him by laying her hand on his wrist.

"Don't rush."

Chuckling, he removed his fingers from the cup. "What? Is there a tea ceremony for alleviating hangovers?"

She plucked the top off a small china pot, allowing a stream of amber honey to drizzle from the imbedded spoon. When the rivulet thinned to a golden thread, she flicked her finger across, breaking the string momentarily.

She slipped her finger into her mouth and sucked away the sweetness. "We could make up our own ceremony."

Ariana dipped the top back into the pot, then lifted the honeycomb-shaped end again, dripping sweetener into his tea.

"A little sweetness and a little spice?" she offered.

He hummed, then silently watched as she added honey to her own tea. She removed the cups from the tray and slid it out of the way, positioning his tea in front of him and drawing hers closer. Folding her legs completely beneath her, she pulled up on her knees. He mirrored her position, directly across from her.

"Close your eyes," she instructed.

He did so without hesitation.

Her heart swelled. *Gotta love a man who takes orders.*

"Now, lift your cup to your mouth, but don't drink."

He peeked long enough to make sure he didn't spill the piping-hot contents and brought the porcelain to his lips. The cup was so white against his tanned, rugged skin. So delicate in hands that Ariana knew could be demanding and rough in the most wonderful ways.

"Take a deep breath."

His chest lifted as he complied then stilled while he held the scent of the tea in his lungs for a long instant.

"The smell alone can clear the brain," he said.

"Wait until you taste it."

He interpreted her comment as an invitation to drink, but she stopped him again with a gentle, "Not yet. Put your tea down."

His eyes remained closed, but he followed her directions, this time without peeking. He adeptly set the cup on its saucer. The corners of his mouth twitched. He wanted to smile, but was valiantly fighting the urge, causing Ariana to grin from ear to ear.

"Lean forward."

He did so as she drank from her own teacup. When the liquid had heated her mouth, she leaned forward to meet him halfway across the table, swallowing when their lips touched, then parted. The taste of the tea flowed from her tongue to his, filling their kiss with the delicious flavor of exotic desire.

When his hands touched her sleeves, she broke the kiss but didn't back away. Their noses brushed as his eyes sprung open.

"Can't I touch you?"

"Kiss me first."

"Can't I do both?"

"You could, but that would be rather…ordinary. Expected. Don't you think?"

He inched back just far enough to study her face. The taste of the tea and the heat of his mouth filled her with the courage to see her fantasy through. She had one week of freedom, as he did. Why fill it with an ordinary affair when they could have a sensual and special liaison? A touch of imagination? A dose of risk? Like in the magazine. Like in the dozens of daring ideas dancing in her head whenever she thought of Max.

"You want the unexpected?" he asked.

"Think about it, Max. When's the last time you really let yourself go? Grabbed the excitement of life and didn't worry about how your adventures would affect your work or responsibilities?"

He shook his head, tilting his face downward so she nearly missed the regretful look that twisted his features.

"That sounds like my brother, not me. Ford is a drifter. He goes where the excitement is, whenever the mood takes him."

"You say that with envy in your voice."

"You think?"

"I'm calling it like I see it. You and I have a bit in common. Both of us have a very clear picture of what we want from life."

"Crystal," he added with emphasis.

"And we've both sacrificed a lot, from a very early age, to get where we want to be. I mean, I left my family on the other side of the country and I work long hard hours every day of the week, but I'm this close—" she pinched her fingers together "—to re-opening Athens by the Bay and making it a real force in the restaurant world. That's what I want—a business that's mine, that people talk about, that they travel to San Francisco just to visit."

"That's a big dream," he said, but not a single syllable suggested that he thought she couldn't make her dream come true.

"Yeah," she said proudly, "but I almost have it. And you know what? It's not always enough."

Max's tongue still tingled from the united tastes of spiced tea and Ariana, and his mind reeled as she made admissions that seemed to come straight from his own heart—from the part he routinely ignored so he wouldn't have to face how empty and predictable his life had become.

"Not always," he agreed.

"Well—" she scooted forward, cradling the teacup in her hands "—imagine we both had a chance to grab some excitement, really drink life. And in the end, there'd be no consequences, no repercussions except a collection of amazing memories."

"Sounds too good to be true."

"I don't think so. I think it sounds too good to pass up. Come on, Max. Have an adventure with me. What do you say?"

8

GOT 'EM.

Leo swung past the dingy narrow alleyway a second time, this time slowing enough to read the license plate. This was too easy. He'd nearly lost them when Forrester doubled back to Chinatown, but despite his employer's low opinion of him, he wasn't stupid enough to blow a second chance at a rather hefty amount of untraceable cash.

Hell, he'd pocketed a cool five hundred just for some misty photos of assorted body parts flailing in the fog. He clucked his tongue as he scanned for a parking place, wondering what the hell the old man was going to do with such screwed-up pictures. But what did he care? He had a wad of twenties in his pocket and a chance to make a hell of a lot more.

He waited for a carload of tourists to pull away from the curb and took their spot. With binoculars, he surveyed the uneven row of old buildings across the street and half a block down. A gift shop. A tea shop. T-shirts. Two restaurants. Cameras for sale.

Luckily, he already knew where Ariana Karas lived. Trading his binoculars for his camera, complete with a telephoto lens, he trained his view to the third floor above Mrs. Lin Li's establishment and snickered. Madame Li might be selling rare herbs and unique tea blends out the front door, but upstairs? Her boarder was selling something entirely more choice. He only wished he'd have a chance at some. But he'd made that offer only to crash and burn. He'd have to settle for the cash.

Red curtains fluttered from open windows.

They were there, all right. And he was going to get them. Mr. Thien Wong owned the porcelain shop across from Mrs. Li. And upstairs, Wong also rented rooms. He hadn't had any vacancies for a long time, but luckily for Leo, his young nephew, Ty, who lived in the room facing the street, facing *her* apartment, loved easy money just as much as he did.

And it wasn't hard to share when more was on the way.

"I SAY, YEAH."

Judging by the widening of her fathomless black eyes and a grin that ever so slowly bowed those luscious lips of hers into a burgundy smile, Max had answered her proposal faster than she expected. The dark lipstick did wondrously erotic things to her mouth, but he still could hardly wait to kiss off all that color.

"Really?" she asked.

"You seem surprised."

"No. Well, yeah, I guess I am. A little."

He shook his head, wondering how the hell she hadn't known how attracted, how enthralled he'd been with her from the first moment they'd met. Max had no idea his self-control and cool demeanor were so effective. Well, he'd certainly need neither of them over the next seven days.

"Good," he said with a grin. "It's not often that I surprise people, except in business. I'm a fairly predictable guy outside the office." He slid the honeypot to his side of the table, lifting the top to slowly swirl the golden contents. He had lots of unpredictable, incredibly surprising ideas about where he'd like to spread the sweet, sticky substance. Places he'd like to lick for the long spans of time required to remove the honey from her sweet skin. "But surprises are good, right? That's what you meant? One week of..."

"...Anything goes?" She reached across the table and dipped her finger in the pot, extracting a stream of honey that drew a thin path across the table leading to her. She dipped her fingertip in her hot tea briefly, then sucked the melting sweetness away, flashing him a devilish grin.

"Anything goes...I like that," he answered.

Her smile bloomed with some secret meaning. He questioned her with a curious glance.

"You said those exact words to me last night," she explained, untangling the long silk robe from around her legs. She fanned the material behind her, exposing her bare knees and thighs.

The warm scents of clove and ginger wafted from the teapot, calming him so he could tap into his practiced restraint. The honey would be good. Later. Mrs. Li had mixed a potent blend he longed to taste, especially when served in the warmth of Ari's kiss. "I said that? Doesn't sound like me."

"Maybe you *do* have inhibitions that need loosening," she suggested, drawing from an earlier conversation he did recall.

"I know I do. I'm all the things you said I am, Ari. Driven. Single-minded." The smile dropped away from his mouth when he admitted, "I can't make any promises to you beyond this week." He had to be sure she understood. Now that Maddie was on her own, the last thing he wanted to do was drag another woman into the craziness that was his life. Max knew he could afford only a brief respite from who he really was—a man who refused to forget what it felt like to be poor and helpless. Or from what he really wanted—the stability only an overflowing bank account and the respect and trust of his colleagues could ensure. Like Maddie, Ariana didn't deserve to be weighted or dragged down by his pursuit of true success.

She didn't deserve his late-night meetings, long phone calls or Sundays at the office. Women like her deserved pampering, attention and damn good loving. At least for the week, he could give her that—and receive the same in return.

She nodded. "I can't make any promises, either. I let my love life stand in the way of my dream once. I won't again. No matter how tempted I might be. But for this week, we can both have it all."

Max wanted to know more about her past, but now wasn't the time to ask, especially since he wasn't sure he was prepared to reciprocate. But they had all week to exchange secrets, to coax out the shadows and triumphs of their lives and loves, to dream and suppose about challenges yet to come. He'd never shared with a woman before—except Maddie. And he had a distinct impression that sharing with Ariana would be vastly different.

His passion for her stirred from a place higher than his groin, and deeper—from his heart. Ariana Karas was a kindred spirit, if one existed for him. How he ever deserved such a twist of fate, he didn't know. And he didn't care. He was grabbing this moment, dammit. This whole week. He suspected he'd never come across such an opportunity again.

"So...you still interested in showing me how this tea will cure my headache?"

His headache seemed to have completely disappeared, though he wasn't about to tell her. Not when showing her would be so much more fun.

Her eyes caught the glimmer of the streaming red curtains billowing from the afternoon breeze. "Oh, yeah. Most definitely."

In sync, they both took long sips of tea, then leaned forward, meeting halfway, mouth to mouth and heat to heat. Flavors mingled on their tongues. Spice. Sweet. Want. Need.

Max gripped the edge of the table, remembering that Ariana had wanted only his kiss before. He judged, by the tension in her arms as she held tight to the table, that she wanted to go slowly—as slowly as two people could go when they impose a time limit on their affair.

The idea was completely foreign, completely outrageous...completely thrilling. Why not? He had nothing to lose. She had nothing to lose. But they both had a world of experiences to gain.

He focused all his attention on learning her mouth. Her teeth were straight and slick. Her tongue bold yet pliant. Her skin was scented with jasmine, and the floral essence mingled with the spiced tea to create a heady combination that surged through his blood. He couldn't stand not touching her. Without breaking the kiss, he slid around on the pillows and pushed the table aside, rattling the teacups.

Ariana broke away, panting but smiling. They were on their knees, nearly thigh-to-thigh. She pressed her palms briefly against his chest and closed her eyes, as if willing both their hearts and passions to slow. Max waited. His gaze followed the bright red piping on her blush-pink robe, around her neck, down her chest, where the edging crossed at a shadowed curve of cleavage, rising and falling with each of her deep breaths. He ached to explore her, pleasure her. Know her.

She smoothed her hands down his arms, as if willing him to keep his raging passion checked for just a moment more. Leisurely releasing the remaining buttons on his shirt, top to bottom, she pulled the material toward her so her hands didn't accidentally brush his chest. She used the sleeve to guide his wrist toward her so she could undo the cuffs—again without allowing even a finger to graze his skin. Once all the closures were undone, she removed his shirt entirely in a quick billow of white. His flesh pulsed with the absence of her touch.

He swallowed. His tongue was thick, his mouth dry. She'd turned to retrieve her teacup, which she cradled with both hands. Swirling the golden liquid, she inhaled the steaming scent, warming her palms on the heated porcelain. After taking a long draught, she set the cup down and shared the heat on her hands with his chest, placing her palms flat so that his nipples touched their hot centers.

The sensation burned like a roaring fire on an icy day. Desire spiked when her lips, equally flamed by the tea, touched the pulse point at the base of his neck. Her tongue flicked a fiery trail across his shoulder, cooling along the way, but stoking his need to touch her, explore her, learn all the things he'd probably learned last night but couldn't remember.

When she started to nibble his earlobe, he'd had enough of remaining still. One hand was clenching the fringe of the nearest pillow; the other was nearly splintering the wood on her table.

"Can I touch you yet or I am I still limited to just kissing?"

She looked up at him with a flash of obsidian fire.

"I'm tempted to say no limits, but..."

"But what?"

Grinning, she reached down and undid the knot of her robe with one quick tug, then clenched the satin together so the material didn't spill open.

"We have all week." She loosened the robe, allowing him a peek of breast, a flash of belly. "And unless you have a condom tucked in your wallet..."

He didn't. He'd never tucked a condom in his wallet his whole life, though his mother had been known to do so when he'd come home from college on the weekends. If not for the freebies he'd gotten at his bachelor party, he probably wouldn't have had any in his apartment last night—assuming they'd used one. Wait, hadn't he gotten nearly half a dozen at the party?

"I have some at my place," he suggested.

She bit her lip. "Uh, no, you don't. Not anymore."

His eyes widened. "We used them all?"

Her laugh, a light sound somewhere between a giggle and a chuckle, inspired the same humor in him. She leaned forward, resting her forehead on his chest, and the scent of her hair and the warmth of her skin nearly knocked the hilarity right out of him.

"So we can't make love," he concluded. "Not right this minute." He ran his hands down her satin sleeves. The friction was slick, liquid. Cool, yet hot. He hardened to the point of pain.

She pressed her cheek to his chest, then bestowed a single kiss just above where his heart pounded hard against his ribs. "Like I said, we have all week."

And there are lots of different ways to make love. She didn't say the words, but he could see the possibilities dancing in her eyes, tugging her lips into a smile, loosening her grip on that robe. And even if the alternatives hadn't occurred to her, they did to him. In erotic detail.

She dug into the couch cushions and extracted a wrinkled magazine.

"What's that?"

"An idea. A fantasy."

"I have plenty of ideas and fantasies, thanks to you. I'm pretty sure I don't need pornography to get me hot with you around."

She laughed as she flipped the pages. "I'm flattered...I think...but this isn't porno." She found the page she wanted, but pressed the open magazine against her to hide the pages from him. "How well do you know the city?"

Max closed his eyes, knowing he wouldn't be able to think very clearly while the only thing separating him from a clear view of her naked body was a scrap of satin and a very tearable magazine.

"I've lived in the Bay Area all my life."

Her eyebrows lifted over disbelieving eyes. She flipped the magazine over so he could see the two-page photo spread. "Have you ever done this?"

Max briefly scanned the photo of a couple making love on the bridge. She flipped a page, then another, then another, flashing images of San Francisco and adventurous lovers at him with rapid speed. She moved to turn the page again, but he stopped her, drawn to a photo in a location he didn't recognize. The scenery, somewhat blurred by a photo effect, didn't grasp him as much as the expressions on the faces of the models.

What did he see there? Excitement? Oh, yeah. Daring? Most definitely. But something more. Something elusive.

"What is this?" he asked.

"I found it on the cable car last night." She tilted the magazine so she could glimpse the picture herself, though he wondered if her wistful expression meant she'd memorized every detail. "It's called Sexy City Nights and it kind of gave me an idea of all I've been missing, all I could discover, if I had the chance. In the city. In my personal life."

He grinned, wondering what that admission cost her, fascinated by how Ariana spoke as if they'd known each other forever—and by how he wanted to return the favor. He wanted to know her. He wanted to live her fantasy. Be her fantasy.

"You're amazing." He tossed the magazine aside, then cradled her cheeks with both hands. "I've never met anyone who can make pure determination sound like spontaneity."

Ariana tried to shake her head, but he held her steady with a soft kiss. She'd admitted a great deal to him—told him a secret about herself that she'd never shared with anyone—partly because she hadn't realized until just last night how much she missed a man's touch. She'd kept herself so busy, thrown herself into her job and her goal so deeply, she didn't have to face the emotional and physical emptiness that haunted her heart.

But being with Max, loving Max, even temporarily, forced her to confront her needs.

"I'm not that complicated," she finally whispered, brushing her lips down the tip of his chin, missing the softness of his mouth at the same time that she relished the roughened feel of his unshaven skin. "I just know what I want. For the first time in years."

"Want to know what I want?" he asked, unable to swallow the laugh that followed, and moving to slide the robe down her shoulders.

"I know what you want," she answered, scooting back, not because she didn't want him just as desperately, but because the front curtain had flown open a little too wide for her comfort. She'd caught her neighbor across the street peering out his window and straight into hers on more than one occasion. Usually, she wasn't doing anything the least bit titillating. Drying her hair. Watching television. Meditating in a roomful of candles.

But this afternoon? In the daylight? Exhibitionism was just fine and dandy for the magazine and under the cover of fog, but she was going to have to ease into that fetish just a little more slowly.

She pulled the robe around her, not bothering with the sash. She wasn't going to be gone that long.

"You're awfully confident," he teased, leaning back into the couch cushions while she made her way around the table.

"That's because I want you, too."

Before tending to the window, she lit another stick of incense and clicked on her CD player. The tune was soft, the volume low and easily drowned out by the sounds emanating from the busy streets below. Holding her robe tightly, she leaned out to catch her wayward curtain and pull it inside so she could shut the old casement windows that opened out over the street.

The minute she grabbed the silk, she felt Max's hand snake around her ankle. Startled, she spun, landing on the windowsill with her back against the center sash to brace her backward tumble.

"What are you doing?" she asked, breathless.

He adjusted the pillows she'd thrown by the window for the nights she liked to read the newspaper and listen to the crowds below. Holding her foot possessively, he settled in comfortably beneath her, kneeling more than sitting as he caressed her arch.

"You have incredibly small ankles."

She was tempted to pull her foot away, but he was doing amazing things to her instep with his hands. Incredible things to her toes with his mouth.

She whimpered. "Shouldn't I come away from the window?"

His green eyes lit with mischief. "No one can see me from outside."

"They can see me."

"Just your back and your hair. Not your face." He kissed a path up her calf, stretching her leg outward so he could suckle the sensitive spot behind her knee—the spot he'd found last night.

She captured her bottom lip with her teeth and bit down, hard, to keep from whimpering again like some forlorn puppy. Like some sex-starved female with a week's worth of pleasure nibbling her flesh.

Clutching the sill to keep from tumbling back, she closed her eyes and willed herself to enjoy the sensation. Max Forrester might not be aware of his fetish, but he flirted with exhibitionism more dangerously than he flirted with her. Not that anyone could see him tugging her belt until it fell away, or inching his way up until his kisses reached her thighs.

Threading her fingers into his hair, she buried her embarrassment in the soft feel of his mouth on her skin. She wanted this. She wanted to break the mold of a conventional affair, create a new, exciting liaison that would belong only to Max and her. She allowed him to coax her legs apart, to touch her, taste her. He parted her pulsing flesh with his tongue and found the center of her need quickly, but alternated his attentions—higher, lower, side to side—so she could no longer anticipate the thrill.

Each lick was a surprise. Each kiss a revelation of need and want and self. The sensation that she was falling had absolutely nothing to do with her precarious perch on the windowsill or her long-held fear of heights. His mouth, his fingers, his groans of utter delight pushed her toward a precipice she desperately wanted to jump from.

So she did. She pulled him closer, throwing her knees wider, taking what he so willingly gave. Below, on the street, the noise of business and tourism and trade muted her enraptured cries of sweet release.

The moment her passion spiraled, Max guided her to the floor, rolling her beneath him on the pillows where he kissed her climax into submission. She shuddered in his arms, shivering as if cold when all she felt was the most intense heat imaginable.

Once she'd regained her ability to form a coherent thought, she asked, "Making love in public turns you on, doesn't it?"

"Never thought about it before." He nuzzled her neck, reminding her that this release had been decidedly one-sided. He was hard against her hip. The thick sign of his desire renewed the pulsing want he'd only just satisfied.

"Well, you need to think about it," she said.

"I will, after we find a drugstore."

She rolled away, grasping her robe together at the same time she gasped for air. This man was potent, nearly overwhelming. She needed to replenish her energy before attempting to return his passionate favor.

And she would. Very, very soon.

The Cheshire-cat grin on his face belied his unsatisfied state. By the twinkle in his lethal green eyes, she imagined he'd been the one to experience the glorious orgasm. "Dress comfortably before we go out."

Walking backward, she disturbed the beaded drape to her bedroom, the musical tinkle startling her. "Comfortably? Do you have a plan, Max?"

He leaned on one elbow, his cheek cradled in his palm. "Oh, yeah. Thanks to you." He relaxed into the pillows and folded his hands behind his head. "We're going to have a sexy city night, Ariana. Just like in the magazine. Only with a Forrester spin."

9

As Ariana accepted his hand, Max swallowed a decidedly appreciative, decidedly male sigh. Men didn't sigh, he reminded himself. They groaned. So he did, loudly, the moment her flesh met his. A breeze from the Bay stirred the scents of the Wharf—a pungent mixture of sea, salt and sunbaked sails—then swirled around this alluring woman who wore a crisp perfume that beat the bitter smells into submission. She stepped out of his car, her long bare legs on stiletto heels appearing first, and challenged him a wink.

"I asked you to dress comfortably," he reminded her, not the least bit disappointed that she'd blatantly disobeyed.

"I'm comfortable. Aren't you?" She smoothed her hands down her skintight skirt, a long swath of black silk with a slit up the thigh that might have showed her panties had she been wearing any.

Her tone had been innocent. Her glance had been innocent. Even her fluttering eyelashes contrasted with her tight red sweater and come-hither smile.

"You're going to be cold," he answered, sure that she knew how uncomfortable she made him.

She threaded her arms into his jacket, her hands skimming beneath the hem of his sweatshirt. "You'll have to warm me up. I told you I needed to know where we were going in order to dress appropriately."

Max leaned in and grabbed her leather coat, helped her shrug into it, then slammed her door shut and engaged the alarm without breaking from her touch. He'd have to let her go in a minute, but right now he was enjoying the sensations entirely too much.

The whole day had been a feast for the senses. First, they'd dressed and toured Chinatown. Ariana introduced him around, showed him the sights few people except those who lived there knew, introduced him to tastes and textures that had nothing to do with sex, but ended up heightening his already charged libido nonetheless. He'd learned a few phrases in Chinese and laughed with the locals at his poor pronunciation. He'd tasted specially prepared squid and sipped the hottest, most potent sake ever distilled. By the time they returned to her room atop Mrs. Li's shop, they were full and drunk and giddy.

With the box of condoms they'd bought at the first drugstore they found, they'd made love on the throw pillows, then fallen asleep, waking just as the last of the San Francisco fog melted into the night.

Max believed it was his turn to show Ariana something she'd never seen, so after a quick phone call and a stop at his house for a change of clothes, they'd parked near Pier 31 and now strolled up the wooden dock toward slip number 12.

The hushed squawk of night-flying gulls and the gentle clang of halyards and rigging accompanied the splashing ocean to create a musical quiet. Ariana shivered and hugged close to him. She was nowhere near dressed for a night cruise on the Bay, but after she learned her lesson in taking his advice, he'd do as she'd asked and warm her.

"You have a boat?" she asked, grabbing his hand

as he stepped over a thick rope lying across the walkway.

"Watch your step. Sort of. The boat is in my name."

She nearly slipped on a wet patch of wood. He was tempted to lift her into his arms and carry her the rest of the way, but was going to have a hard enough time explaining Ariana to his brother who waited for them aboard their yacht, the *Oakland Dreamer*.

Ford would more than appreciate Ariana's exotic beauty, enhanced by her clothes and by the glow of having more than one orgasm in the past twenty-four hours. For a moment, Max wondered how many women Ford had carried onto their boat for a midnight liaison. More than likely, his baby brother didn't even bother to cast off. But Max had more to show Ariana than just the soft bed in the master cabin. He wanted her to see the city, lit up and sparkling against the wind-roughened Bay—the image he'd first seen as a child that had contributed to making him the man he had become.

"I hope you have a lot of energy, mister. Warming me up will be no easy task." Frustrated with her slippery progress, Ariana tugged off her heels, wincing when her feet met the chilled wood.

"Maybe you're going sailing with the wrong brother, then," Ford claimed from above.

Max glanced up to find Ford leaning over the flybridge of their sixty-foot cabin cruiser, securing a line Max knew must be important though he had never taken the time to learn much about his floating investment. So long as Ford brought the boat back from charter fishing trips and pleasure cruises in good working order, Max normally ignored the operation all together. Ford wasn't making them any richer, but he was happy and out of trouble, which was the reason Max bought the boat in the first place.

He nodded at Ariana, indicating that this was the brother he'd warned her about and that if she had a clever comeback to his insinuating insult, she was more than welcome to return the volley.

"You must be Ford," Ariana said simply, obviously not wanting to play into their brotherly feud.

Ford slid down the ladder to the main deck, looking every bit the modern-day pirate with his windblown, shaggy blond hair and twinkling eyes. He'd obviously shaved for the wedding that never happened this morning, but he still managed to exude pure rogue charm wearing nothing but a wetsuit. He held out his hand when Ariana came closer. "I'll be anyone you want me to be, sweetheart."

Ariana stuck out her tongue as though she was gagging. "How about being original? That line was banned for overuse about ten years ago."

Zing. Max grinned while Ford faked an injury to the heart, then took her hand and helped her on board.

"My brother told me you were different."

"I said *special,* Ford. Ariana is special. Mind your manners. Your job is simple. Take us out on the Bay. You can do that, can't you?"

Ford chuckled and helped them both aboard. In minutes, the dual engines roared to life, a growling echo in a marina normally silent at this time of night. Max freed the bow from its mooring then joined Ariana.

She stood on the aft deck, hugging her leather coat close to her body as Ford eased the boat out of the slip and puttered slowly toward the Bay. Max had two choices: pretend to know what he was doing enough to help his brother maneuver out to sea, or practice what he did know—warming Ariana. He motioned for her to come in closer to the cabin where the wind, already slashing against them before they even left the protection of the marina, would be buffered by the fiberglass walls.

"You could have told me we were going out on the Bay," she mumbled, only half complaining as he pulled her full against him.

"I didn't want to ruin the surprise. You're not afraid of the water, are you?"

She smirked. "Isn't my fear of heights enough? I love the water. More specifically, I love looking at the water, sailing on the water. But let's not forget that San Francisco Bay is shark-infested."

He leaned down and nibbled her neck, blazing a path across her throat where his chin rubbed against her cleavage. "So I've heard."

She pulled back enough to meet his gaze. "Maybe this boat is shark-infested, too. You should see the look in your eyes. I'm feeling somewhat like shark bait right now."

"You don't look like bait. You look utterly amazing. And you taste...fantastically...delicious." With a sharklike strike, he returned to nipping her neck. She laughed and tugged his hair, the sound of utter freedom urging him. Rewarding him. He shrugged out of his jacket and pulled it around her shoulders. He no longer needed the extra layer to keep the chill away.

He was hot, and getting hotter. The slap of the wind and the spray from the waves as Ford increased the boat's speed into open waters acted like agents of fire, spreading the sensual conflagration until he was sure he'd burn with wanting. He wanted to make love to her. Here. On deck. With the rock of the waves to give rhythm to their instinctual tempo.

And he would. As soon as he got rid of Ford.

They kissed and teased and touched and played until his brother slowed the boat and idled the engine. When Ford climbed down from the elevated helm, he took one look at Ariana and Max as he headed toward the bow to lower the anchor and smiled from ear to ear.

"Lady, I don't know what you've done to my brother, but keep doing it. I haven't seen him this loose since he was six and sniffed a little too much Elmer's glue."

Max socked Ford in the arm as he passed, causing Ford to howl with unbridled laughter.

"Damn, bro! You haven't hit me since you were six, either. When I was a pain," he said to Ariana, conspiratorially angling his hand across his mouth as if Max couldn't hear him, "he used to steal my allowance. Then he'd invest it. T-bonds. Blue chips. I'm not kidding."

Max put his arm around Ari's waist, hoping to shield her somehow from the truth of his carefully planned and executed childhood, which led him to his carefully planned and executed life. "We had quite a portfolio by the time I turned sixteen, if I remember," Max reminded him.

"Yeah, well..." Ford hedged, not the least comfortable with any point conceded, however true. "I would have rather had baseball cards and bubble gum."

"Baseball cards and bubble gum wouldn't have

paid for a nice chunk of our college tuition,'' Max chimed, shaking his head. He loved his brother, he honestly and truly did, but he didn't understand how they could have been raised in the same household. Ford was in a constant state of laid-back, roll-with-the-flow relaxation while Max was in a perpetual siege of uptight, concentrated energy. At least he normally was. With Ariana around, he was acting more like Ford—and he was beginning to recognize the appeal.

Ariana obviously sensed an argument brewing, so she stepped between them while cuddling closer to Max. ''Now, that would depend on the baseball card, wouldn't it? People pay millions for some of the rare ones.''

Ford's smile defined smugness.

''Don't encourage him, Ari. He's a hopeless nomad as it is. This boat is the only way I keep him in one place.'' Max glanced out at the expanse of Bay and ocean that was his brother's workplace. ''Relatively speaking.''

''Yeah, well, if you didn't finance my boat, you wouldn't have your own midnight charter cruise and captain, would you?''

''Actually, we could do without the captain.''

Ford scanned the sky, which was clear and full of bright, twinkling stars. Not a cloud in sight. Max grinned. He was not in the least bit qualified to captain this boat, but he did know the basics—how to untie the moorings, where to find the life jackets, how to turn the engine and bilge pump on and off, and how to use the radio to send an SOS. He doubted he and Ariana would get into any trouble he couldn't handle on his own.

At least, none of the nautical kind.

"I was just leaving," Ford murmured. He lifted the top of a padded seat and pulled out a life jacket, shrugging into it and securing the straps. "I stocked the galley after you called. Ariana, I have a big, warm, hooded sweatshirt hanging on the back of my door. Down the steps, first cabin on your right."

Ariana thanked Ford, then grinned at Max, smirking at the smoothness with which his brother had dismissed her. Yet without a word, she braced her hands on the railings and made her way out of earshot. He and his brother did have a few things to talk about.

"I had a great time at your reception," Ford said by way of getting straight to the heart of the matter. "Got the phone numbers of two bridesmaids and several of Maddie's cousins."

"Then why aren't *you* using the boat tonight?" Max quipped, not entirely sure which part of the truth he wanted to tell his brother.

Ford shook his head. "Who says I'm not already through? But that's not the point, Maxie, and you know it. Who is she?" He gestured toward the cabin. "And where the hell is Maddie?"

Max groaned, then went to the stern to help Ford release the WaveRunner from its compartment to aid his departure. "I don't know where Maddie is, but she's the one who told her parents we eloped. She called me last night, just around midnight, and left a message on my car phone."

"On your car phone? Why didn't she call your house?"

"I suppose she wanted to make sure she was long gone before I even knew she was missing."

"Mom and Dad are going to be disappointed. They really liked Maddie."

"She's not dead, Ford. She's gone to find herself. Her lie just bought her some time. I respect her ingenuity."

Ford nodded, obviously impressed himself. "Man, but the shit's gonna hit the fan when Randolph and Barbara catch on. You should have seen them this afternoon. They played king and queen of the kingdom to the hilt."

Max laughed. His brother had guessed a long time ago that Maddie and Max's decision to marry wasn't because they were in love. Ford had accepted their plan in his usual, laid-back style, somewhat entertained and resigned to watch the events unfold. "If you came to more family gatherings, you'd know that Randolph and Barbara Burrows play king and queen all day, every day. I'm sure Maddie will return ready and willing to handle them. I just hope she realizes she'd better get back here in a week. I can't disappear forever."

"Sure you can, bro. You just *won't*. Too many deals brewing."

"I'd say 'I have my goals, you have yours,' but that would only be half-true," he quipped. He heard Ari closing a door belowdecks and remembered he had better things to do than berate his brother for the lack of direction in his life. "Don't come back until after sunrise, okay? *Long* after sunrise."

Ford climbed onto the WaveRunner and held out his hand to accept Max's keys. Although it wasn't legal, Ford lived on the boat. If Max wanted him out of the picture for the night, he'd have to relinquish his car and house in trade.

"You still haven't told me who this Ariana is," Ford reminded him while he unzipped a pocket on the life jacket and stuffed the keys inside.

Max considered his next words carefully. What could he tell his brother about this woman that wasn't an intimate secret? A sensual confidence? Wasn't that all he really knew about her? Those things private and personal and not open to discussion?

"She's someone I know," Max answered. "Someone who in one day has shown me more about me…more about this city…than anyone I've ever known. I just want to return the favor."

ARIANA HEARD THE ROAR of a smaller engine and climbed back on deck in time to see Ford skim away on a personal water vehicle. Max was nowhere in sight. Except for the quiet hum of the retreating vehicle and the lapping of waves against the fiberglass hull, the night was soundless.

Then she heard music—cool jazz sung in dulcet tones and accompanied by a saxophone so mournful, she closed her eyes while the emotions rocked her. A moment passed before she heard Max climb down from the helm where he'd tuned the onboard stereo.

He looked somewhat disappointed that she'd done as Ford suggested and traded her tight red sweater and sleek leather coat for his battered but surprisingly clean San Francisco Giants sweatshirt, size extra, extra large. The soft fleece swallowed her from shoulders to just above her knees, and though she'd rolled the sleeves at the wrist, her hands were still hidden in folds of gray. But she was warm. And judging by the hungry look in Max's eyes, she was about to get warmer.

"Where's Ford?" she asked, knowing he was gone but fishing for information about the timing of his return.

"I threw him to the sharks."

"Ha, ha. I saw him on the WaveRunner. That's incredibly dangerous, you know. Going out in a wet-suit at night. He'd be hard to see."

"Ford lives for danger, Ari. And he's good on that thing. He's just going back to the dock, where he'll take my car to my house and live a life of luxury, which he won't appreciate. He'll come back in the morning. We have all night."

She couldn't help but smile as she smoothed her hand across the polished railing, then stretched her fingers toward the sky. "*This* is luxury. The night. The chill. The waves and wind and rush of being alone just far enough from the city where we won't be disturbed, but close enough to see the skyline in all its glory."

"Good point. What are we waiting for?"

Max took her hand and led her around to the bow. They were moored just off Sausalito, close enough to see the Golden Gate, yet far enough so they didn't hear the hum and whir of cars and trucks crossing over. The skyline rose like a mountain range of twinkling shadows. Transfixed by the awesome beauty of the city, Ariana barely felt him lead her back onto a cushioned seat until she was cradled in the V between his thighs.

"This is wonderful, Max. Thank you."

"No. Thank you. It's been a long time since I saw the city from here."

The wistful, sad timbre of his voice clued Ariana

that more was at play here than the glittering lights
of the skyline.

"How long?"

Max pulled in a deep breath, pausing while his gaze
became lost in a tunnel of time. "I was nine. My
grandparents had come from Florida and took Ford
and me on a night cruise, a real tourist tour. We'd
been living with my aunt and uncle in Palo Alto and
I think they needed a break."

"Where were your parents?"

It seemed a natural question to ask, but the moment
the query tumbled from her lips, his chest stiffened.
She turned in time to meet his tortured gaze.

"You don't have to answer," she said quickly, regretting that she'd delved into some painful part of
his past. Not because she didn't want to know everything about him—she did. She just hadn't expected
to stir up such an obviously difficult memory. "I
didn't mean to pry."

She grabbed his wrists and pulled his arms tight
around her. After a moment, he relaxed.

"It's okay. My parents were back in Oakland. My
father drove a cab for a living and he'd been shot by
a robber."

"Oh my God! Max, I'm…"

"He was okay, but he couldn't work for over a
year. Mom was a public-school teacher and she had
to quit her job to nurse him. There wasn't enough
money to feed and clothe two growing boys, so we
made the rounds of the relatives."

Ariana's heart pumped hard, bleeding for the little
boy who'd known a poverty and loneliness she
couldn't imagine. Though her family had been stifling

to her as she approached adulthood, her time as a child had always been secure.

"No wonder you're such a driven businessman."

Max chuckled, but the cadence lacked any real humor. "You don't know the half of it. My grandparents told us on that boat tour that if my father didn't return to work soon, we'd have to go to Florida with them. They acted like Walt Disney World and sandy white beaches would make abandoning my parents all okay."

He buried his face in her hair, inhaling the scent of her shampoo. She nuzzled back into him. He was baring his soul to her. She wanted deeply to offer at least a silent comfort.

"I was so angry. You should have heard me—nine years old—negotiating a loan with my mother's father, estimating the costs of supporting two boys and then adding on the expenses of a family on disability and welfare. I even knew the current interest rate. He was so impressed, he brought us back to our parents and took out a second mortgage to help us out."

Ariana's chest eased at the sound of pride in his voice. "So you started working to pay back the debt yourself."

"I sold newspapers, ran errands, collected bottles for deposits and, later, cans for recycling. I learned about investing and the stock market from a banker whose shoes I used to shine. By the time I was in high school, I knew the big bucks were in real estate. So, here I am."

Yes, here he was—a man more complicated than she'd ever imagined, driven by the wounds of poverty and separation from his family to make an indelible mark on the financial world. She could now understand why a marriage of convenience to a wealthy, connected woman would fit with his needs, both professional and private.

"Here we are," he said. "We've got the view, each other, no money worries and six days to enjoy the city."

Realizing he sought to restore the playful mood of their excursion with a lighthearted tone, she rewarded him with a seductive shimmy.

He responded in kind, sliding his hands down her silky skirt. The heat from his palms contrasted completely with the icy wind slithering through the thigh-high slit. He then ventured beneath the hem of the sweatshirt, bunching the material as he inched up past the waistband of her skirt. With the cold air swirling just on the other side of the thick cotton, his hands exuded pure fire. His fingers teased the lower swells of both breasts. When he skimmed her nipples, they were hard.

He sucked in a breath, moaning his pleasure at her arousal. "You're very cold." Nuzzling her neck through her hair, he plucked and pleased and toyed. In one afternoon, he'd learned exactly how to touch her. Exactly how to start that liquid pounding between her thighs, that rainbow euphoria that made her lose her mind.

Then tonight, he'd let her glimpse into his heart—into his soul. A powerful aphrodisiac she couldn't—wouldn't—fight. Nestled in his lap, she could feel the strain of his erection against her back. Memories of making love to him on his balcony—facing the view, with him deep inside her—kicked up her response to his gentle foreplay another notch. If he continued, she'd come right here, right now, with him doing no more than touching her breasts and kissing her neck.

"You're...making me...hotter," she said between gasps.

"That's the idea."

Moisture trickled down, kissing her inner thigh. "Too hot."

"No such thing."

She scooted off the seat long enough to turn around and sling one leg over his thigh, her slit flashing open. "Sure there is. God, Max. I'm so close and we're both still dressed."

He inched through the opening of her skirt. "How close?"

His cat-in-the-cream smile and bold touch made her suck in her breath. She'd made a tactical error if she'd thought that admission would slow him down. Instead, he blazed a trail straight to the center of her need where his wind-chilled fingers met the wet desire he had stirred. She remained standing, half straddling him while he probed and parted her sensitive flesh.

"You feel so slick," he told her.

She braced her hands on his shoulders. "Max..." She could say only his name. Couldn't he see what he was doing to her? Did she really have to expend the energy to form a response?

"Mmm," he answered for her. "Feels good, doesn't it? So soft. So silky. So wet."

When he eased a finger inside her, she bit down a gasp. He played her with deep thrusts, rhythmic and round, rotating his touch until her knees started to buckle. He bunched up her skirt, exposing her to the elements in one cold flash, then yanked her fully onto his lap and pulled down the sweatshirt's hem.

Not once did he stop touching her, stroking her. The sweet pressure built. She couldn't wait.

"Come on, honey. Let me see you lose control. Here. With the city behind you. And me inside."

She shook her head, fighting the flashes of color, raging against the orgasm that was only moments away.

"You're not inside," she protested.

"I will be, sweetheart. Later. But right now I'm not stopping long enough to put on a condom. Not unless you want me to stop. Do you want me to stop?"

With a second finger, he stretched her, prepared her, forcing her over the edge. "No, Max. Don't... stop. Don't..."

She bit down hard as the convulsions began.

"We're in the middle of nowhere, Ari. Let me hear you. Let me hear you come—just from my touch."

She shook her head, but it was useless. Useless to deny Max anything he wanted. Anything at all. She gasped and shouted, unintelligible sounds, sounds she'd never heard spill from her own lips.

Yet judging by the look on Max's face as she collapsed into his arms, the payoff for her surrender would be worth the price.

10

HE DONNED PROTECTION in the time it took for her to catch her breath, then he was inside her, sex to sex, warm and wet and as wild as the Bay rocking the boat.

She folded her knees up on the padded bench, drawing her closer; him, deeper. She set the tempo, but he gauged the depth. Splaying his hands on her cheeks, he pulled her mouth to his for a long, tongue-clashing kiss.

''Again. Please.'' She tossed her head back, crying his name. The sound tugged at him, sexually. Spiritually. She wanted him. Here and now and for no other reason than because they sought and gave pleasure, together. No ulterior motives. No hidden agendas or looming financial payoffs. Hard to the point of pain, he throbbed for release. He could think of nothing else, feel nothing else.

She sat up fully, nearly breaking their intimate link. The cold air stabbed at his bare skin. He clutched her bottom and pressed her down, sighing as heat enveloped him again.

He blinked, realizing he'd closed his eyes in preparation of the rapture. When he glanced up, she was watching him intently, her hands still bracing his face.

She rode him to her own primitive beat, her smile

growing as passion stole his sight. But when he felt the end looming, he stole back the driver's seat.

"My turn, honey. Let me hear you again." He twisted, adjusting their position until he could go no deeper. She gasped and cried when he touched just the right spot.

Her shudders pushed him over the edge, into a place where only heat existed. Where the air was hot and thick and nearly impossible to breathe. He came with a mighty roar, his voice echoing across the water. He pulled her down for one last thrust, then held her steady, capturing her mouth as their orgasms ebbed and the cold air returned.

This time, she quaked from the cold, so he bundled her as best he could and carried her downstairs.

In minutes they were nude and nestled beneath the covers of the feathery, queen-size bed. With the cabin lights dimmed, only the stars and the shine from the city through the windows lit their gentle embrace. Shivers came in one strong wave along with chattering teeth that made them both laugh, which led to tickling, which led to touching, which led to one long, soft kiss that eventually drew them into a comfortable quiet.

"I can't believe we've made love this much in less than twenty-four hours," she said, snuggling closer and laying her cheek on his chest. "I'm not usually this horny."

"Must be the company you're keeping," he said smugly.

"No doubt." She twisted her fingers into the patch of hair at the center of his chest. "We're good together. I don't think that happens very often."

Max bit the inside of his mouth. No, it didn't happen very often. Not to him, anyway. Yeah, he'd had flings and affairs from time to time, but never like this, never with such an irreverent, carefree attitude. Never with pleasure and pleasing being his one and only agenda. Even in college, he'd chosen the girls who had the right connections, who could give him an edge in his classes with their knowledge or who could get him invited to the right parties with the right people. Not that he wasn't attracted to them or didn't like them individually, he just decided attraction and basic interest weren't enough.

Even when Maddie had pointed out the shallowness of his actions, he'd chosen to ignore her words. Ariana understood him, fully accepted what it was like for him to have to claw his way to success.

And judging by the way she'd responded, she was okay with his past. And why wouldn't she be? She'd worked her way up much as he had. But she'd also been married once. She hadn't completely ignored her personal life as he had. He couldn't help wondering how any man could have let this remarkable woman go.

"What about your husband? You must have been good together or you wouldn't have tied the knot."

She squirmed, but didn't pull away. "We were very attracted to each other. Rick was a sexy man. Unfortunately, you can't build a marriage on sex."

"Good thing for us," he said, wincing at the callous sound.

But she didn't hesitate to agree, which increased the sting tremendously. "Exactly. And you know, as sexy as he was, he never paid attention to what I liked. I was a virgin when I married him. He barely had to touch me and I'd come. After a while, my orgasms weren't so easy. But he wasn't interested in working on anybody's orgasm but his.''

Max pulled her closer, amazed and pleased that she could speak with such candor. ''The man was a fool.''

She nodded, snuggling closer. ''Yeah, that's what I figured out. Recently.'' Her mouth twisted into an ironic grin. ''But by that time, I'd closed myself off to trying a relationship again. All I wanted was work, work, work. Success and more success. Now I've just about gotten what I want...and I've got you, to boot. For now.''

Her gaze actually softened when she voiced yet again the temporary status of their affair. He expected something different—a touch of regret, a bit of melancholy. He swallowed a tiny taste of bitter disappointment.

''Don't worry, Max,'' she reassured him, misinterpreting his frown. ''When I make a deal, I stick to it. You and I, we're great. But you have a whole life out there that I don't fit into. Connections and cotillions and million-dollar deals. In a way, I'm sorry Maddie and you didn't work out. She'd probably do that part real well.''

''Don't sell yourself short, Ariana. You're a beautiful, charming, intelligent woman. The San Francisco elite would find you as breathtaking and fascinating as I do.''

''Is that before or after my fourteen-hour day at the restaurant? When I come home smelling like a kitchen? Or worse, a bar? How breathtaking and fascinating is the woman who just got done mixing your Absolut and Evian? Come on, Max. Let's not weave some dream that won't come true.''

Max's logical side conceded her point. They were

from different worlds. Unfortunately, his ambitious side knew too well that clever, intelligent, determined people could successfully cross the chasm from one world to another. They only had to have the know-how. The desire.

"You and I are living proof that all sorts of wild dreams can come true," he pointed out. Moments ago, he'd subscribed to the same determination—to keep their affair temporary and brief. But the more he thought about it, the more he resented the emptiness in his personal life. Just this once, he wanted to try something new. Someone new. Ari.

The flash of apprehension widening her gaze told him now wasn't the time to make the suggestion. He'd bared his soul tonight and gained insight in the process. Insight into both of them.

"You're right." She eased her hand down his chest and explored until she found his sex. "We can create wild dreams." She encircled his shaft with her fingers, teasing below with her nails as she disappeared farther beneath the covers, trailing a path of open-mouthed kisses over his nipples, down his abs, across his hips. "And they'll come true, all right."

"Ari..."

"Shh..." She let the elongated syllable tease his moistened tip with her hot breath. "No more talk, Max. No more talk."

He couldn't deny his desire any longer. They'd have time for conversation later. Much, much later.

FORD RETURNED TO THE BOAT after 10:00 a.m. By then, Ari had changed into a complete sweat suit and Max had served her a breakfast feast of cheese and canned fruit on a blanket spread on the bow. Ari guessed they'd slept two hours, maybe three. But she'd managed to make sure that each waking moment was filled with either sex talk or sex play and no more discussion of her marriage, her goals or her plans for the future.

Especially any future that included Max, enticing notion that it was. Even Ariana, a consummate dreamer, knew that some things were out of her realm. She couldn't stand to set herself up for something so pie-in-the-sky as a serious relationship with Max only to be crushed when his schedule, her schedule, his obligations, her obligations, his career, her career, clashed and warred and destroyed the special connection they'd formed in the past two days. She was too close to having everything she wanted to let love get in the way. Again.

She guessed that Max's canceled marriage was forcing him to take a long hard look at his life. She respected and admired him for latching onto the opportunity to take stock and consider changes, but dammit, she couldn't afford to let his self-assessments alter her own decisions.

When Ford docked and began his washing and gassing and whatever else seamen did to ready their vessels for the next cruise, Ariana considered saying goodbye to Max and grabbing a cab home. Despite spending an entire glorious night on the open sea, she had a strong urge for space. For just an hour or two.

Max beat her to the punch. "Why don't I drop you off at your place to pick up a change of clothes and take a nap? Then I'll take you out for dinner. Somewhere I'll have to pay some obscene amount of money to get us in since we have no reservations."

"Like a date?" she asked, tamping down a sigh of relief.

"Not *like* a date—a date. Flowers. Small talk. Good wine. No plan. No expectations. Just...fun."

The man was a master of true romance and he had absolutely no idea. Good. Because if he had any inkling of the power he wielded and he decided to seriously train his sights on her beyond this week, she'd be a goner for sure.

"Sounds wonderful. What do you feel like? Italian? French?"

He shook his head, taking her hand as he helped her off the boat and they said goodbye and thanks to Ford. "Let me surprise you."

She hooked her arm around his waist as they walked, suddenly regretting that she'd entertained the idea, even for a minute, that her decision to be with Max might be wrong. When he concentrated his decision-making powers on her, the results were always incredible.

"It's worked quite well so far," she said.

"Oh, yeah. That it has."

MAX DROPPED HER OFF at the front of the tea shop, kissing her sweetly on the knuckles before she bundled her red sweater and silky skirt into her leather coat and watched him drive away. She hesitated, smoothing her hand against her cheek, imagining his scent still lingered on her skin.

"You're in trouble, girl," Mrs. Li announced the moment Ariana entered, engaging the jangling brass bell her landlady had strung along the top of the door.

"Excuse me?"

Ariana couldn't imagine what she could have done

to offend Mrs. Li. They had no standing rules against having a lover stay over and, technically, Max hadn't slept in her apartment anyway. Glancing around the shop, she realized that, except for the three women sitting in the back sipping tea out of earshot, she and Mrs. Li were speaking privately.

"That look on your face. Trouble. Good trouble, but trouble anyway."

Ariana bit her lip and started to walk toward the stairwell in the back until she realized she'd have to pass by Mrs. Li's friends who were clucking over some article in the newspaper. In her experience, that trio was just as intuitive and nosy as the woman who collected her rent. They imparted advice at absolutely no charge, and until today, she hadn't minded hearing their perspectives.

She really didn't mind so much now, either. But she'd rather deal with one matron of experience than with four.

She moved to the counter where Mrs. Li was opening small wooden drawers filled with dried herbs, extracting some with a tiny metal spoon into a paper cup. "Is there such a thing as good trouble?" Ari asked.

"You answer me."

Ariana replayed the past two days in her mind, then went back farther. She thought back to the minute Charlie had deceived her about Max and his wedding, to her discovery of the magazine. The sexually charged flirtation in the bar. The surprise in Max's drink. Deception. Erotica. Illegal drugs. All trouble individually.

All wonderful when meshed together to result in her union with Max.

"Yeah, trouble can be good. Very good."

Mrs. Li nodded, pursing her lips sagely. "That's why trouble is trouble. Can be very good or can be bad. You have to be smart to keep it good." She tapped a finger to her temple and shook her head. "Not smart with your head." She lowered her finger to her chest, still tapping. "With your heart."

Ariana rolled her eyes. She wanted to keep her heart out of this. Her heart usually got her in the bad sort of trouble. "My heart isn't the organ I trust most."

Mrs. Li returned to scooping herbs into her cup. "If you don't trust your heart, it'll get broken for sure."

"It's been broken once. It mended."

Shoving the last drawer closed, Mrs. Li poured the herbs into the center of a sheet of butcher paper, then folded and tucked until she'd created a perfect square packet of her medicinal mixture. "Was it really broken? Or just bruised?"

"I loved Rick," she insisted. Rick had been Mrs. Li's boarder before Ariana came to live with him. Their landlady had baked the wedding cake they'd eaten after returning from the courthouse ceremony. She'd been there for Ariana after Rick left, nursed her with kind words and strong teas and sometimes-silent company until the pain of his abandonment subsided. How could she not know how devastated she'd been?

"I didn't say you didn't love him. But Rick never loved you back, not the way he should have. It's the man's love that truly tears the woman's heart apart, and vice versa."

After labeling the small square packet with a wax pencil, Mrs. Li tossed the order in an out basket and answered the summons from the back table to join them for tea. She invited Ariana, but Ari smiled and shook her head, too intrigued by Mrs. Li's words, too distressed by what might be happening between her and Max, to subject herself to chitchat with the ladies. She accepted the newspaper they were finished with and escaped upstairs as quickly as politeness would allow.

She tore through her living room quickly, not wanting the throw pillows and windows and tea sets to remind her of the decadence she and Max had enjoyed. She removed her borrowed sweats and tossed them into the mountain of dirty laundry on top of the hamper in her closet and dashed into the shower.

She was going to enjoy tonight. She was going to enjoy tonight without thinking about the damage Max could do to her—and she to him—if either of them succumbed to falling in love.

MAX PARKED IN HIS GARAGE, but closed the door from the outside so he could collect his newspaper and Saturday's mail from the boxes outside his front door. His brother, who'd stayed at his home the night before, had no interest in the goings-on of the world if they weren't printed in San Francisco's newest rag, *The Bay Area Insider,* so he wasn't surprised to see two days' of the more conservative *Chronicle* littering his porch.

After unlocking the front door, Max flipped through his mail while lights flickered on and off as he made his way into the kitchen. As expected, Ford had left a mess. Normally, Max didn't care. But he was all too aware that he'd given his housekeeper the week off, so he shoved his mail in the appropriate cubbyholes and collected the dirty dishes from the table, rinsed them then stacked them in the dishwasher.

He found *The Bay Area Insider* spread out on the kitchen table that looked down on the rest of Russian Hill through a wall of crisp windows. In a vain attempt to compete with the more venerable, long-established competition from the *Chronicle* and the *Examiner,* recently merged, the upstart newspaper was rife with gossip, innuendo and downright lies. Max scanned the headlines. *Castro Club Owner Hot for Young Customers. Cruising the Embarcadero for Rich Sex.* Then, atop a hazy picture of two people doing something rather up close and personal outside in the fog, he read, *Prewedding Jitters?*

Max lowered himself into the nearest chair. He forced his gaze away from the photograph—away from the shape of a woman with long, black hair—away from what appeared to be a bare breast peeking out of the heavy fog that curled over an outdoor balcony—and read the short square of text below.

San Francisco won't be shocked by lovers taking liberties out in the open, but they might raise an eyebrow if they knew which respected, high-powered real estate broker poised to tear into a city monument in the next few weeks was entertaining a lady obviously not his fiancée on Friday night. The shot's not clear, but the activity is. We can see the Forrest through the trees, er, fog. Can you?

Holy shit.
Max read the caption again. Then again. He'd com-

mitted the words to memory by the time he registered the sound of the telephone ringing. His answering machine clicked on before he reached the receiver. The red number indicating the message count changed from twenty to twenty-one.

Hesitantly, Max lifted the receiver in time to hear Charlie's voice pleading, "...you gotta call me, Max, before anyone else—"

"Charlie?"

"Max! Damn, where the hell have you been?"

"As if you didn't know," Max snapped. Despite his horror over the caption in the paper, not to mention the photo, hazy as it was, he still hadn't forgotten that Charlie's deceptions might have led him to the brink of this current catastrophe.

Max knew his own balcony when he saw it. And all that dark hair? Ariana's undoubtedly. Hell, he recognized her breast. How could he not when he'd spent hours upon hours in the past two days exploring and enjoying every inch of her body?

He swallowed, forcing the stone of rage that had formed in his throat to settle in the pit of his stomach.

"I called her restaurant," Charlie explained. "No one answered."

"They're closed for renovation. You know that, you lying son of a bitch."

Charlie groaned. "Her number's not listed."

"Get your ass over here, Charlie. Now."

Max's mouth twitched as he heard the click on the other end of the line. Almost hypnotically, he dropped the receiver back into the cradle and watched the red number blink and blink. How many of those calls were from Charlie? How many from Randolph Burrows? Or his other investors? How many from the owners of the Pier, the owners he'd enticed to the property? These people were new-monied, upstart capitalists who were more concerned with using this project to buy their way into San Francisco respectability than with the cash they'd make on the development deal. They were a cautious group that had nearly balked at the first sign of controversy over Max's brilliant plan to convert the Pier, currently used for commercial fishermen, into a classy, slick collection of high-end nightspots and shops to compete with the carnival-like tourist draw at Pier 39.

Max backed away from the answering machine. If his ass was going to be chewed out on recorded cassette tape, he sure as hell wasn't going to listen without Charlie there to suffer every word with him. He might not have been on that balcony with Ariana if not for Charlie's lies.

The rustle of newsprint alerted him that he was still clutching the paper in his hand. He scanned the photograph again. Must have been Friday night—the night he couldn't remember.

He couldn't see her face, but he knew it was her. He slumped into a chair by the window and looked closely. He saw a hand. His hand. Palm flat against the Plexiglas that surrounded his balcony.

Closing his eyes, Max tried to stir up one memory, one sensation that might make this scandal-in-the-making worthwhile. He shook his head, realizing he didn't need to remember the deed to justify the risk. He had the past two days of clear and crisp memories to erase any inkling of regret.

He felt no repentance for one instant with Ariana, erotic or otherwise. But he sure as hell didn't want to lose this deal.

And he didn't want to lose her. Not until the appointed time, when he'd have no choice. They'd agreed to a week-long-only affair, and though he'd already entertained several schemes to see her well beyond the deadline, she'd made it more than clear last night that she preferred they adhere to the original plan. He shook his head and plopped into a nearby chair. When she saw this picture, she might call off their affair right here and now.

When she saw this picture...

Max dashed to the phone, then realized that, like Charlie, he didn't have her phone number. He did, however, know the name of Mrs. Li's shop, so after a quick call to Information, he waited for the connection to go through.

"Lin Li, Herb Shop," Mrs. Li answered in her brisk, efficient English.

"Mrs. Li? This is Maxwell Forrester, Ariana's friend."

The woman chuckled lightly. "More than a friend, I think. What can I do for you? Interested in more of my tea, maybe?"

Max was tempted to ask her if she had one that included strychnine as an ingredient—something he could serve to Charlie—but he didn't know the woman well enough that she'd understand his black humor. He did, however, understand that if he was going to ask her for a favor, he'd better make it worth her while.

"Actually, yes. I'd love to put together some gift baskets for my office staff. Four of them. Assorted teas, cups and such. I'm not sure what goes into one..."

"That's my job. Four baskets. I can do them for tomorrow. How much you want to spend?"

They negotiated a fair price and once Max was a few hundred dollars poorer, he finally asked Mrs. Li to give Ariana his phone number and instruct her to call him right away.

"Sounds important," Mrs. Li commented without bothering to hide the sound of her worry.

"Yes, ma'am. It is."

"Then I'll bring her the message immediately."

Max hung up and stalked upstairs, showered in record time, then stood in a towel scanning his closet while he wondered what the hell he was going to do. Charlie's knock on the door answered his dilemma for him.

"Get in here."

Charlie walked in sheepishly, a copy of *The Bay Area Insider* neatly folded and clutched beneath his arm. He shut and locked the door behind him.

"No reporters lingering on your doorstep," Charlie announced brightly. "That's a good sign."

"It's Sunday. Give them time. Fix me a scotch and then meet me upstairs. I'm going to get dressed."

He was slightly concerned that Ariana hadn't yet called, but only fifteen minutes or so had elapsed since he'd given Mrs. Li the message.

"You're going out?" Charlie sounded as shocked as Max was, but Max waved away his surprise and bounded up the stairs. He'd promised Ariana a real date. And judging by the chaos she was about to be plunged into, he owed her at least that much. He would pick some out-of-the-way, very dark restaurant—one not likely to be frequented by anyone who would understand the barely hidden references in the photograph's caption.

He'd donned his underwear and a pair of pants by the time Charlie came up with his drink.

"There's nothing in here, is there?" Max asked, eyeing his supposed friend warily to gauge his reaction.

All he saw was confusion. "I put ice.... Isn't that how you like it?"

Max swirled the gold liquid. Ice clinked against the crystal. The sound was way too innocent and delicate for the situation.

"Yeah, it's how I like it. Doesn't mean you wouldn't add a little something...like on Friday night maybe? Something to make me relax. Take a certain restaurant owner home? Miss my wedding to your cousin...a wedding you didn't approve of?"

Charlie looked down at his hands, then once he'd strung Max's hints together, shot him an incredulous, offended glare. "What the hell are you implying?"

"Someone slipped me a Mickey on Friday night. Probably laced my beer...that beer *you* insisted we stay late to have."

"Max, man, I'm a schemer, I admit that. I told Ariana a few choice lies to get her to make a move on you...but I wouldn't put something dangerous in your drink. What if you were allergic?"

Max weighed Charlie's logic with his obvious sincerity and the fact that Charlie had a list of allergies as long as the real estate listings he represented in northern California.

"Well, someone put something in my drink."

Charlie hesitated. "Ariana, maybe?"

"No. It happened before she made me that flaming

drink, probably before she arrived. Whoever did it knew I was going to be at the bar. And only *you* knew that.''

''It wasn't me, Max.''

Max glanced at the newspaper, now spread across his bed. Who would have been watching him? Training a camera lens on his balcony at some time after midnight? The fog had obviously been thick that night. It's not as though a neighbor or some passerby could have seen what was happening and alerted the newspaper. A chill ran up his spine and tingled the damp ends of his hair.

Someone had been following him. Was *still* following him? As he toured Chinatown with Ariana? As he pleasured her on the windowsill or made love in the open waters of San Francisco Bay?

The phone rang and Max grabbed the receiver without considering that anyone but Ariana might be on the other end.

Ariana sounded winded and drowsy, as if Mrs. Li had roused her from sleep. ''Max, what's wrong?''

''Do you read *The Bay Area Insider?*''

''The newspaper?'' She sighed, sounded more relieved than she would in a few moments. ''Yeah, usually. Not today. I was taking a nap. Mrs. Li said you called. I thought something was wrong.''

''Something is wrong. Do you have a copy of today's edition?''

He heard a rustle of newsprint, and though he called her name, she'd obviously taken the receiver away from her ear to grab the paper.

''Here,'' she said once she returned. ''I picked up Mrs. Li's copy on the way up. What's in here that...''

Her voice died away before he could explain or warn her. "Oh...my...God."

"Ariana, relax. No one can tell who you are. The caption doesn't even allude to your name at all. Just me."

"Oh...my...God," she repeated. "That's...oh...my..."

With a high-pitched beep, she disconnected the call.

11

"DAMMIT! SHE HUNG UP!" Max clutched the phone until he heard the casing begin to crack, then slammed the impotent device on the bed. "I can't imagine what she's thinking right now."

"Call her back," Charlie snapped.

"I don't have her number. And I don't want her landlady asking more questions. Ari must be embarrassed enough by this as it is."

"You don't need to call her landlady." Charlie scooped the cordless from atop the comforter. He punched in *69, the code that would identify the number of the last person who called. He pressed the number for automatic redial and handed the phone to Max.

"You're way too clever," Max groused. "You sure you didn't orchestrate this mess I'm in?"

"Why would I, Max? I'd never hurt Ariana this way. The two of you were supposed to be happy together." When Max scowled at his friend's magnanimous, lofty intentions, Charlie grunted and amended his claim. "I don't want you to lose the Pier deal— or my part of the commission."

As the phone trilled with unanswered rings, Max accepted that Charlie wasn't lying—this time. Sure, he didn't want Max and Maddie to marry and make what Max now knew would have been a horrible mistake for both of them, but Charlie would no sooner jeopardize a deal than he would cut off his right hand.

"She's not answering," Max announced, swearing as he disconnected the call. "I need to see her."

He shot back into his closet, pulled out a crisp, white, button-down shirt, glanced down at his khaki slacks and blanched. Two days ago, his predictable, classically *GQ* casual wardrobe wouldn't have bothered him. But now he'd tasted the flavors of the unexpected, savored the richness of living outside the box. Potential scandal or not, Ariana would never forgive the old Max if he went charging into her apartment as the man he was before.

He dug a little deeper, hissing out a triumphant "Yes!" when he found the laundry Ford had left at Max's house after the engagement party he'd hosted a month ago. He'd had it all cleaned, of course, and, knowing Ford, he didn't even realize his clothes were missing. Well, Max would put them to good use.

He took a long swig of his scotch before unbuckling his pants to change.

"You can't leave now, Max. We've got damage control to plan. Have you checked your voice mail? Have any of the investors—"

"I don't give a rat's ass about the investors right now, Charlie. But if you're so concerned, go to the kitchen to check my machine and then call in to my office voice mail." He gave Charlie the password. "But do it quick. I'll be ready to go in ten minutes, and you're coming with me."

"With you? To see Ariana? I'd think I'm the last person she'd want to see right now."

Max shook his head. "Second to last. But you're coming. You're going to tell Ariana—and me—the whole story of your involvement in Friday night. Then you're going to help us figure out why someone was taking pictures of us.''

''Will I make it out alive?''

Max turned away and dressed, his expression doubtful. He'd known Ariana Karas intimately for only two days, but he respected her Mediterranean temperament and her justification in letting loose on both of them. He and Charlie were about to charge into the den of a wounded lioness, but they had no other choice. He had no other choice. He'd agreed to let her go at the end of the week, but not like this. Not with hurt and betrayal between them. And maybe not at all.

ARIANA READ THE CAPTION again. She'd lost count of exactly how many times she'd read the words—sometimes silently, sometimes aloud—but the exact number didn't matter. Little by little, she'd broken through the haze of her disgrace and realized she was being used.

Not by Max, but because of him. Maxwell Forrester was the ''Forrest'' the writer referred to. In her opinion, that reference wasn't the least bit clever, but the words were certainly laced with disdain and mockery. Obviously, Max had been working on some controversial development deal, something that angered someone enough to want to dig up dirt and print it in San Francisco's newest daily. But had it angered that someone enough to drug Max and set him up for that picture to be taken?

Either way, she'd been caught in the cross fire.

The risk you take, she told herself, *when you mess with a man outside your world. A rich, famous man.*

But hell, it wasn't as if Max was a movie star or a political figure. He was a businessman doing his job. Was someone out to make him look bad and screw up one of his business deals? Or was this just someone's sick idea of a joke?

Well, Ari wasn't laughing.

She tore through the pages of the newspaper for the name of the editor and the number to the newsroom and ripped the masthead out. No use calling today, a Sunday. She certainly didn't want to deliver her oration on yellow journalism to an answering machine. But they'd hear from her tomorrow. Maybe in person.

And then what? They'd know who that breast belonged to, wouldn't they? Maybe they'd print another picture, one that showed her face, run a story about her and her restaurant and her family.

She crumpled the torn piece of newspaper and pitched it across her tiny kitchen into the sink. No righteous indignation for her.

But where did that leave her and Max?

She had no time to consider the big question; her thoughts were interrupted by someone knocking on her door. Just short of pounding, the raps were insistent, hurried. Desperate.

Max.

She shot up from the table, then slowed down as she crossed into the living room. She tightened the sash on her robe. The pink one. The one Max had seen earlier. The one he'd loosened as she sat on the windowsill so he could kiss her ever so intimately. She let the beautiful image flow over her, reliving the sweet sensations, when the knocks started again. She wouldn't fall into his arms for comfort, she promised herself. She wouldn't. They'd already become much closer than she planned in only two days. Maybe now was the perfect time to call things off and escape relatively unscathed.

Maybe…

After a quick peek through the peephole, she flipped the locks and opened the door.

"You got here fast," she said by way of greeting. She'd already turned away and plopped onto the couch before she realized that Max wasn't alone. Charlie sheepishly followed Max inside and shut the door.

"Well, look who it is," Ariana said as she pulled her lapels closer and eyed Charlie from head to toe. "Benedict Arnold, reincarnated just in time to ruin my life."

Max bit back a chuckle and, deep inside, breathed a sigh of relief. If she still had her sense of humor somewhat intact, he still had a chance to repair the damage.

"I asked Charlie to come and explain what happened Friday night."

"I didn't drug Max," Charlie explained quickly, picking that detail out as the most important. Max believed him. Charlie wouldn't do something so dangerously reckless.

"Then who did?" she asked.

Max moved around the coffee table and sat on the cushions beside Ariana. The scent of incense still hung heavy in the room; the scent of sweet jasmine still radiated from her skin. He ached to take her hand in his, walk her through this situation gently, but she clenched her fingers in a tight ball on her lap and impaled him with an impatient look.

"We don't know," he answered.

"Look," Charlie said, practically pleading. "Maddie just asked me to keep Max at the restaurant long enough for her to make her getaway."

"Maddie!"

Max and Ariana shouted the name in unison.

"You *knew* Maddie was going to bolt?" Max asked, needing clarification. He and Charlie had spent the car ride to Chinatown reviewing the business-related messages Max had received and discussing how they were going to ease this situation for Ariana. They hadn't had a chance to go over the facts beyond that. This revelation certainly hit Max unprepared.

He'd assumed Madelyn's disappearance had been spontaneous, but now that he thought about it, that didn't make sense either. Weaving the tale of the elopement to cover her trail had been brilliant—and required preplanning. He'd known Madelyn for many years and spontaneity wasn't her forte. She'd made quite a few stupid decisions when backed into a corner. "Since when? When, Charlie? When did you know?"

Max was about to stand when Ariana laid her hand on his knee. The gesture wasn't calming, as she'd obviously intended. But it sure as hell stopped him dead. A surge of something electric—a mixture of relief and desire—shot from her warm palm directly into his skin. He fell back into the cushions, his anger inoculated.

"About a month ago," Charlie answered once he realized he was safe and didn't need to shoot for the door. "Maddie wanted to call off the wedding, tell you she'd made a huge mistake, but she didn't know how."

"That's bull!" Max insisted. "Maddie could tell me anything. She knew why we were getting married. Hell, it was her idea! It's not like she was going to break my heart."

"No, but she might have broken up the deal for Pier Nine. At that point, you'd sunk a lot of capital into it and, like it or not, her father and his bank control most of your investment funds. She was afraid that if she called off the wedding, something she knew you'd agree to, Uncle Randolph would take it out on you by torpedoing the deal. She knows how much the Pier means to you."

Max pressed his lips together, silenced by the truth. Luckily, Ariana had questions of her own to fill the void while he mulled over Maddie's collusion in this potential catastrophe.

"And how did I play into this?" Ari asked. "Did Maddie handpick me?"

"No. You were my idea. I've spent the past two years watching Max stare at you, watching him pretend he wasn't salivating every time you walked through the restaurant or stopped at our table. I just figured I'd play matchmaker. That simple. I had the opportunity. I took it."

Charlie stepped forward and knelt by the coffee table, as close to Ari's feet as he could. "I swear on my mother's grave. I just wanted the two of you to be happy."

Ari's ebony eyes narrowed. "Is his mother really dead?" she asked Max, obviously wondering how to gauge his friend's sincerity.

"Since he was twenty," Max answered with a bittersweet grin. "And from what I hear, she was a very good woman."

Ariana's lips twisted into a reluctant grin. "I'm sorry for your loss." Then she grabbed his shirt at the chest, twisting the cotton around her hand. "But if you ever lie to me again, Charlie Burrows—if that is indeed your real name—I'll light you up the same way I do my Flaming Eros, understand?"

Charlie grinned and stood, smoothing out the crinkles in his shirt. "Yes, ma'am."

"So, now what?" she asked, breaking her eye contact with Charlie to lock an expectant stare on Max.

"Now *I* apologize," Max said. "I didn't mean for your picture…"

She pulled her robe more closed. "Let's not talk about the picture, okay? Like you said on the phone, no one can tell it's me." She squirmed and her gaze darted at Charlie, then back to Max.

Charlie didn't miss the hint. "Maybe I should leave you two alone. I'm going to drop by Uncle Randolph and Aunt Barbara's house. See what they know."

Max nodded. None of the messages on his machine were from Randolph Burrows. Ten calls were from Charlie. Two were from his secretary, who read *The Bay Area Insider* daily, and accurately read through the hidden meaning in the caption, but angel that she was, assumed the picture was a fake. Several others were congratulatory messages from wedding guests who'd gotten word of the elopement and couldn't make the ceremony since the bride and groom weren't going to be there. None yet from any investors or the owners of the Pier. The picture had done no damage—so far.

"Tomorrow is Memorial Day," Max reminded them. "Most offices are closed. We have until Tuesday before we can really find out what's going on.

Most of our investors are loyal to the *Examiner* and the *Chronicle*. They won't read *The Bay Area Insider*. It's too young and hip. But they'll hear the news as soon as they get back to their offices.''

''What do you want me to say when they start calling?'' Charlie asked.

Max had absolutely no intention of going into the office and handling this himself. Yes, it was probably the prudent thing to do. But since Maddie had gone to all that trouble to create a week-long alibi, he wasn't going to screw things up with Ariana when he still had a chance to make things right.

''I'm going to get the hell out of town like I'm supposed to be. That's what you tell the investors. How could it be me in the picture if I'm in Hawaii? On my honeymoon?''

''You have a very distinct balcony, Max. These people know real estate.''

''Then tell them the picture could have been taken a long time ago...before I owned the house. Or maybe it's Maddie and me. Our privacy was invaded and we're outraged. I don't care what you tell them, Charlie, just keep things as calm as you can for twenty-four hours. We'll check in then.''

Max turned to Ariana and joined both her hands with his. ''That is, if we're still a *we*. You still want to see the city with me?''

With a hint of a smile, Ariana bit her bottom lip, imbuing Max with a surge of power and relief that had his heart beating hard against his chest. He didn't know what was happening to him. He'd been putting business and profit ahead of fun and pleasure since he was a child—a child old enough to realize that being poor meant you had little control over what happened to you. He'd been single-minded in his pursuit of wealth, his parents and brother being his only soft spot—a spot that eventually grew to include Maddie and Charlie. And now Ariana. And with Charlie newly married and Maddie exploring the world, Max felt the emptiness in his heart with magnified intensity. He couldn't let Ariana just slip away.

She grinned at him now with a smile half wicked, half resigned. "I think we should concentrate on the outlying areas of the city—those secret spots no one knows about—don't you?"

She still had her sense of humor. She still had her sense of adventure. The woman was unstoppable once she set her mind to something. If he could help it, he wouldn't hurt her again.

The door clicked closed as Charlie departed. A thousand separate concerns ricocheted through his brain. The first was the possibility that the photographer who had caught them on the balcony continued to follow them and had more pictures to share with the press—more ammunition to convince his investors that Max had faked his marriage, was a liar not to be trusted, was a cheat unfaithful to his wife. Who knew what other sickening spins someone with an agenda could put on his affair with Ariana to impugn his development deal?

But at the moment, Max didn't care. The moment his lips pressed against Ariana's soft mouth, the worries of his world dispersed in a puff of smoke.

LIKE TEENAGERS ON THE RUN, Ariana and Max stuffed a few essentials into one small bag, rented a convertible in her name, just in case, and took to the highway. As they pulled onto Highway 1 approaching the Golden Gate, Ariana leaned back into the buttery leather seat and closed her eyes, allowing the stiff wind to buffet her face. By the time they'd passed the tollbooth where people on the other side paid to enter the City by the Bay, she wasn't the least bit concerned with newspapers or scandals or real estate or bare breasts peeking through fog and Plexiglas.

Anticipation for her next adventure with Max overrode any and all negative thoughts. She didn't even succumb to that unstoppable sensation of falling she usually experienced just thinking about going across the bridge, much less actually doing it. Max was doing amazing things to her fear of heights—first on the balcony and then at the windowsill. Max did amazing things to her, period.

She didn't remember ever feeling so free, so avid and impatient for adventure, since she'd boarded the plane to California all those years ago. She'd been wide-eyed and open to all experiences then. Ready to cast off the chains of her upbringing. But marriage to Rick had slowly taken most of the fight out of her— forced her to narrow the scope of her vision and energy on career goals only. She'd done damn well for herself, but now she clearly saw all she'd missed.

With Max, she fantasized she could take on the world—and win. If only she could keep Max around for longer than a week. Shaking her head, she forced the thought away. *Not today,* she insisted to herself, knowing that following that train of thought would lead to maudlin conclusions she didn't want to face.

Instead, she focused on the thrill of doing something new, something she'd wanted to do for years. As a restaurateur and bartender, she'd been invited to attend tastings and festivals in nearby Napa and Sonoma Valleys. The tourists in her restaurant raved about the beauty of the wine country, but she'd never had the time to go. Maybe she'd never made the time. Maybe she hadn't wanted to experience the rolling hills and fertile farmland by herself or with only business on her mind.

Thanks to Max, now she didn't have to.

"This is wonderful!" she shouted over the roar from the road. "I can't believe you booked us at a private winery. I've never even been to one that's open to the public! Are you sure your friend won't rat you out to the newspapers?"

"Phillipe?" Max shifted the car into fifth gear, then settled comfortably into a fast cruising speed. "He doesn't give two flips for American politics if it doesn't affect his business. He came to the States from France five years ago with a box of grapevine cuttings and a dream. I was the real estate agent who found the winery he bought and built up. People don't do that anymore, you know."

Ariana nodded. "My great-grandparents did, but that was a long time ago. They turned a plywood seafood stand into one of Florida's premier Greek restaurants."

"Your family runs a restaurant in Florida?" he asked, apparently surprised. "Why didn't you stay and run their place? Not that I'm not glad you came here."

She rewarded his considerate comment with a sweet smile. "If I'd stayed in Tarpon Springs, I would never have made it beyond hostess. Women in my family don't make important decisions or give commands—or generally do anything that requires public acknowledgment that you have a brain."

"Which is why you left," he guessed.

"Two weeks after my nineteenth birthday. Don't get me wrong. I love my parents and my brothers. And I really didn't want to go. I admire the sacrifices my great-grandparents made. My parents, too. But, even though they raised me, they couldn't give me the respect I wanted."

Max's frown deepened as her story progressed. "They'll have no choice but to give you that respect once you've made a real splash with Athens by the Bay."

"That's the plan." She hated that Max could read her so easily, but then realized his own background gave him precisely the insight to understand the ferocity and breadth of her goal.

Hard work. Sacrifice. Ingenuity. Those three qualities had turned her great-grandparents' American dream into reality. And she'd learned that those same three elements could go a long way, no matter the goal: restaurants, wineries...true love.

She shook the thought away, choosing to watch Max drive instead. He gripped the steering wheel at two o'clock with his right hand, his left arm was casually draped on the door while he toyed with the side mirror. His choice of clothing surprised her, but she thanked whoever or whatever was responsible for this fashion inspiration. The silky, slate-blue shirt fluttered in the wind, allowing her elongated glimpses at his bare chest. The material pleaded to be touched, smoothed by a woman's palm. And who was she to say no? As soon as they got off this bridge, she was going to find out just how soft and slick that shirt was. And the skin underneath.

They drove across without another word, but the

minute Max passed the exit to Sausalito—the small artist colony where they'd been docked the night before—Max asked a question that kept her desire to touch him in check.

"Did you and your husband ever take excursions out of the city?"

He glanced sidelong before putting his gaze back on the winding road, shifting and braking in smooth, fluid motions. He sure managed to mention her former marriage quite a bit. She didn't mind as much as she thought she should. The pain of Rick's rejection truly had faded to near nothing.

"Rick and I left the city all the time. He was a musician. He played gigs from Oakland down to L.A. We even went to Reno a few times."

"So you probably saw more outside the city than you did within?"

She laughed at his assumption. "What I saw was the inside of a ratty van and even rattier clubs. I won't even discuss the hotel rooms. Being a musician is an exciting adventure—for the musician, but not for his too-young, too-inexperienced wife. After a while, I stopped going with him. A little while longer and he was off to Seattle, then Nashville without me—for good."

"So you hung out with your uncle at the restaurant while he was on the road?"

Ariana's heart swelled. Max always seemed to plug right into her, know things about her before she told him. And he showed more concern with how Rick had abandoned her before the marriage was over, somehow knowing that had hurt the most. By the time Rick had left her the divorce papers, the worst was over. The damage had been done long before.

"Stefano was great to me. He gave me a job, taught me to mix drinks, let me experiment with the food. By the time Rick left, Stefano knew I was ready, willing and able to take over for him." She stared at her hands, wringing them softly in her lap to keep her emotions at Bay. She'd *so* wanted to run her parents' restaurant in Florida, but they'd made it undeniably clear that the legacy belonged to her brothers. She could work for them as her sisters did, but she'd never run the show. So she'd left for California to find something to call hers and hers alone.

"The distraction of working was much appreciated and couldn't have been better timed," she concluded.

Max switched his right hand for his left on the wheel, then reached over and cupped her hands in his. "But running Stefano's restaurant turned into more than a distraction, didn't it? More than just a temporary means to take your mind off the sorry state of your life?"

The double meaning wasn't lost on Ariana. Their weeklong affair was supposed to achieve the same goal—provide a brief distraction to take both their minds off the sorry, lonely state of their lives. Scandal or not, she could feel their liaison changing into something much more serious, much more binding than she'd ever imagined.

She tried to pull her hands out of Max's grasp, but he held tight. After he turned his eyes back to the road and allowed a self-satisfied grin to curl his lips, she gave up trying. He wasn't going to say another word about it and he wasn't going to let her go. He'd given her plenty to think about, plenty to hold on to and, luckily, they had a long drive ahead.

12

RANDOLPH BURROWS DRUMMED his fingers atop the grainy black-and-white photograph, grimacing when smudges of ink transferred from the newsprint to his fingertips. He pulled a handkerchief from the breast pocket of his blazer and wiped away the grime.

Too late for that, he mused. He was deep in the grime of scandal, deeper than he'd ever planned to be. Having Max Forrester followed should have produced some evidence of his ill-bred character *before* his daughter got hurt. He'd put a private investigator on his trail the day after Madelyn announced the engagement. He'd found nothing but the vague possibility that Forrester was having an affair with the owner of an ethnic restaurant on the Wharf. The rumored affair had been proved real by this picture, but too late. Madelyn had already run off, obviously humiliated.

Randolph had thought the photograph to be unusable, with the quality so poor and his daughter on the lam. He'd only paid the punk with the camera in hopes he'd find something more damning while he followed Maxwell and his Mediterranean mistress around the city—something Randolph could use privately to force Maxwell Forrester out of their deal, now that the wedding was off. He had no idea his amateur paparazzi would take his money and then sell the indistinct photograph again to the newspapers.

This was supposed to be a personal matter.

With precision, Randolph withdrew a pair of scissors from his desk drawer and cut out the picture, then placed it in a manila folder that he slid into his briefcase. He needed to find his wayward photographer and yank in the reins. He'd accept nothing less than loyalty, even if he had to pay a hefty price to get it. Somehow, Leo Glass had figured out that there was more at stake in this operation than his daughter Madelyn's honor or a few thousand dollars.

He stood, then tapped the button on his intercom. "James, bring the car around. I'm going to the office."

"Oh, no, you're not!"

Barbara fluttered into the room and poised at the corner of his desk, much like a butterfly alighting on a flower. She held a hat in each hand as if she was just coming into his study to ask his opinion on which one would look better with the flowing blue frock she wore. Damn, but she was one handsome woman. He couldn't help but grin at his wife's expression, a mixture of chastisement and humor. She would do her best to keep him from working today. She always did.

"It's a bank holiday," she pointed out, as if he somehow didn't notice that the stock exchange was closed and he hadn't had to rise before dawn to beat his staff to the office, as was his weekday ritual. "I've made reservations for us to take a cruise on the Bay and Magda has packed a beautiful picnic lunch. We're meeting the Andersons at the Pier in an hour."

"Darling, that sounds delightful, but I have an urgent matter I must attend to."

"Nonsense, Randolph. How long has it been since we've gone off on a romantic excursion?" There was a slight pout to her grin, but only a slight one. She'd long ago perfected the exact dose of solemnity to add to her sensuous smile in order to get her way. "I suppose all this wedding planning and Madelyn's elopement has me waxing poetic, but we're not getting any younger. So tuck your business away until tomorrow. I allowed you to take your meeting with Charles over that Pier investment yesterday. That's enough money talk for this holiday weekend."

With that, Barbara leaned across the desk, kissed his cheek and retreated, nodding approvingly at the large-brimmed straw hat as she left, deciding entirely on her own. Some retreat, he thought wryly. She'd won that argument, just as she'd won so many others.

No use canceling the car since they were indeed going out, but he did have one phone call to make. He walked around his desk and shut the door. Barbara was still in the dark about their daughter's humiliation and self-preserving deception and he planned to keep her there until he had no other choice. He didn't blame Madelyn for running off and concocting that elopement story to buy some time to save face. In fact, he found the scheme incredibly clever, more so than he'd expected from his daughter, who was naively but endearingly honest and idealistic.

And he couldn't disavow his hand in her naiveté. He'd shielded her from the ugliness of the world, as was a father's right, a father's duty. But Maxwell Forrester had shattered that safe wall he'd built around his one and only child, and for this he would pay.

Randolph certainly had no intention of scuttling the Pier deal at his own expense. But it seemed someone else had that agenda or, more than likely, it was just this upstart newspaper longing for a local scandal to increase subscriptions. Once he had the situation back under his control, he'd push his philandering, almost son-in-law out of the deal to make him pay for what he'd done to Madelyn.

And from what he could see from the photograph and caption, he'd pay with a lot more than money.

ARIANA LEANED AGAINST the wall in the hallway, allowing Max to work the key to her apartment. It had been a long day—a glorious day. She was still giddy from the windblown ride back from Napa Valley, still dizzy from the bottle of Phillipe's special wine they'd drunk just before leaving. With a borrowed blanket and a basket of cheeses and fruit, they'd found a secluded spot at his winery, shaded from view by rows of blooming vines and fat bunches of grapes. Actually, since Max planned to drive, she'd done most of the drinking. Not enough to get certifiably toasted, but enough for him to nearly seduce her amid the golden Chardonnays. A seduction she had, with great difficulty, rebuffed.

No more making love out of doors, he'd proclaimed, then promptly tried to reverse his wise decision. Since they'd left the city, she'd tried not to think about the photo in the paper and all the potential problems the scandal could cause. He'd resisted her myriad questions regarding who would have the motive for such drastic measures or who would have known how to find them at his house, much less on his balcony. He hadn't wanted to discuss his troubles, preferring to concentrate on enjoying the here and now with her. So they'd toured the winery, watched hot-air balloon races, even attended a wine tasting on board a train that snaked around the lush hills of the valley. But they'd made love only at night, in the guest house Phillipe prepared for them. And during the glorious sexual byplay, they'd barely spoken a word. They didn't need to. He knew what she liked and vice versa.

On the way out to Napa, Max had invited her—oh, so subtly—to consider the possibility that their affair didn't have to end when the week did. That the "distraction" their liaison was supposed to provide could be altered into a real relationship. The offer was so tempting. The potential payoff so great. But if Ariana had learned one thing about relationships, it was that they required sacrifices, compromises, give-and-take. And while she didn't mind enjoying the ebb and flow of sharing Max's life this week, she held tight to the belief that she wouldn't be able to be so magnanimous once she went back to work next week.

Knowing Max, hearing about his rise to prosperity, made her want her dream even more. She'd coaxed a few stories out of him over the past two days, tales of his search for success. She'd heard about how by age twenty-one, he'd graduated with a degree in business. How by age twenty-three, he'd earned his real estate license and was buying and selling properties while he successfully completed his MBA. How he'd met the right people, made the right contacts. And this deal with the Pier—the one he really didn't want to talk about because of its connection to the embarrassing reference and picture in the newspaper—if he managed to pull it off, he'd be a millionaire several times over—his ultimate goal since childhood when he'd realized his family was poor.

Her dream was decidedly smaller, simpler, but no less important. She didn't just want a restaurant to call her own—she wanted a showplace. A unique dining experience that travel guides never overlooked, that the food critics raved over, that the locals enjoyed with the same fervor and comfort as the tourists. She couldn't imagine attaining her goal without selfish, single-minded pursuit—much as Max had employed earlier in his career.

Fact was, he was at the uppermost point of his rise toward success. She was just starting the climb.

"Are you coming inside or does this hallway have some charm I'm missing?"

Ariana turned toward his voice and blinked. The lights inside her apartment were all on; the television was tuned to the cable station playing a very sexy movie she'd been wanting to see. She could even hear the whir and crackle of her microwave making popcorn. He'd obviously gone inside while she stood in the hallway thinking. She felt like an idiot, but the aftereffects of the wine took the edge off her embarrassment.

"I guess I drank more than I thought," she said, sheepishly brushing past him and tossing her purse onto the black lacquered chest.

"You're probably tired. We didn't sleep much last night."

She swept a kiss over his lips before heading toward her bedroom. "No, we didn't. But I'm going to seriously relax tonight, just as soon as I change into my pj's."

"Our relaxation techniques don't usually include sleep," he said, barely managing to cover a yawn with the back of his hand.

"No, they don't."

He arched an eyebrow. "Maybe tonight we'll try something new."

Max shook his head, amazed, as she smiled with anticipation and disappeared beneath the beaded doorway. He could always depend on Ariana to try something new with him. Something exciting. Something so special he was finally convinced there could be more thrills found with a good woman than with a closed deal or a jump up to a new tax bracket.

And she'd convinced him without trying. In fact, he figured that if she knew the effect she'd had on him, she'd run for cover. He'd had absolutely no trouble keeping Ariana focused on the present during their excursion—no arguments when he declared they wouldn't talk about anything serious and only enjoy the scenery, the view and each other. Unlike any other woman he'd ever met, Ariana was content to keep their interaction casual. And he knew why. If things remained casual, she could more easily say goodbye.

Pushing his disappointment aside, he went back into the kitchen to listen to the microwave. They'd made a deal. She'd stick to it. But would he? Keeping his competitive spirit at Bay was hard enough—keeping his growing disappointment under wraps even harder. Not to mention his pride. The realization that he wasn't irresistible was about as easy to swallow as an unpopped kernel of corn.

He didn't often cook for himself or for others anymore, but he could microwave popcorn with the best of them. He timed the intervals between pops, shutting off the power before one kernel got scorched. Gingerly, he pulled out the piping-hot bag and searched for a bowl.

He was just about to shout a question to Ariana when he heard her curse from the bedroom.

"Ah, damn!"

He looked around the corner from the kitchen to the living room, just in time to see her emerge with an overflowing armful of laundry.

"What's wrong?" he asked.

"There's nothing like the real world to intrude on your fun. I have to put a load in the washing machine."

"Can't it wait until tomorrow?"

She shook her head and expertly maneuvered to the door despite the hefty laundry blocking her view. "Not if I want clean underwear."

Max shot to the door and opened it for her, then blocked her exit with his arm. "Who needs underwear at all?"

She sighed. "Great question, but I do like the option. Mrs. Li lets me use her laundry room downstairs, but she needs the machines on Tuesdays. My day is Monday and Monday is nearly over. I'll only be a minute."

He let her pass, but not without bestowing one long, rather wet kiss to show her what she'd be missing if she didn't hurry. She broke away, groaning as she ducked beneath his arm and made her way down the hall to the stairwell. "Promise more kisses like that and I'll make it back in thirty seconds."

She'd twisted the knob and propped open the stairwell door with her foot before he could assist her.

"I can keep *that* promise," he said.

With a smile, she disappeared. Max remained in the hall, staring at the door as it swung closed. He could promise her kisses. He could promise her good loving. Hell, he could promise her the world—and deliver—if she'd let him.

He made his way back to the kitchen, shaking his head. He couldn't let her go. His nature didn't allow for such sacrifice. His heart would no longer accept the emptiness he'd lived with so long. Not now that it knew the fullness Ariana put there, whether she'd intended to or not.

He thought about Charlie. So far as he could tell, his best friend was an expert on two things—selling real estate and finding him the perfect match. He'd schemed brilliantly to bring them together. Ariana's honest, adventurous spirit effectively broke down a wall around his heart that Max hadn't realized existed. But once Ari was inside, as she now was, he couldn't let her out. She understood him. Admired him. Wanted many of the same things he did.

And therein lay the problem.

As he pulled open the hot bag of popcorn and poured the contents into the large plastic bowl he found in a cabinet above the refrigerator, he realized only two things stood in the way of keeping Ariana in his life.

First, the photograph. He assumed the whole incident was somehow set up, starting with the drug in his drink. Perhaps someone had been following him for weeks, learning his habits, watching for weaknesses they could exploit into a scandal. Common sense dictated that someone trying to sink the Pier deal had schemed to make him vulnerable and then planted a photographer to capture the results on film. They'd probably searched for shady business dealings or other dark secrets to exploit, and finding none, decided to concoct their own. Ariana's presence, the timing of their liaison, was nothing more than an accident, a twist of fate.

A wonderful twist, Max thought, popping a buttery morsel into his mouth.

Considering all angles and all possibilities, Max knew there was nothing he could do to stop this potential scandal. He had no idea if more pictures would surface or if his investors would react negatively. For all he knew, the whole matter would die a quiet death.

He also had to consider the second barrier to bringing Ariana into his life for the long haul—Ariana herself. Her dream was a big one, her goal admirable. But Max knew firsthand the sacrifices that had to be made to make a business work. He could adapt. So she'd work long hours. So did he. So they'd see each other mainly when he came to the new restaurant. He could live with that.

Couldn't he?

Scooping up the bowl and grabbing two long-neck beers from the fridge, he set their feast in front of the television and considered the past two years, when he'd watched Ariana from afar, talking to her only briefly. When she was working, she was entirely focused, consumed with her attention to detail, ensuring that each and every patron of her establishment felt pampered and served and welcome. Every customer was a good friend, every employee family. She was excellent at her job—the best he'd seen in such a casual setting—one reason he'd been drawn to Athens by the Bay in the first place.

Was it fair to ask her to divide her focus? Now, when she was so close to achieving everything she wanted, everything she deserved?

The thought made him pensive. Frustrated. Annoyed as hell. He twisted open a beer and grabbed a handful of popcorn, stuffing his mouth and chewing. He was a genuine son of a bitch. Still selfish. Still self-absorbed. Still willing to bulldoze his way into her life for the sake of his own needs.

Because, dammit, he wanted Ariana in his life, no matter the cost.

ARIANA WATCHED MAX from the corner of her eye, then glanced back at the screen. The sexy, romantic comedy had zero effect on whatever black mood had descended on him while she was downstairs separating the whites from the delicates. He'd barely spoken three words, and while he didn't recoil from her arm entwined with his, he didn't invite any other affection. She tried to console herself with the fact that he was tired and that tomorrow, the first business day this week, could result in a crisis over his Pier deal, but she sensed that his mood had more to do with her.

"Max, what's wrong?"

He turned to her slowly. "You don't want to know." He blew out a frustrated breath. "I'm sorry. I'm being a jerk." He chugged down the rest of his beer, now undoubtedly lukewarm since he'd done nothing but clutch the bottle for the past half hour. "I'll get over it. I'm exhausted."

"I do want to know. Is it the picture? Are you worried there might be more? Worse things could happen, Max. Embarrassment never killed anyone."

He turned and clutched her hands, a smile fighting with the frown that had reigned over his face since she'd returned. "You've got a great attitude. I want you to know that I'm sorry for involving you."

"You've apologized a hundred times, Max. You know I don't blame you. That's not what's wrong."

He glanced aside, then back at her. He wanted to tell her—she could see the signs. Deer-in-the-headlight eyes. Mouth slightly agape.

He wanted to but he wouldn't. Instead he stood, grabbed the empty beers and the depleted bowl of popcorn and retreated to the kitchen. She shook her head. Maybe he was right—maybe she didn't want to know.

Maybe she already knew and didn't want to face the crossroads they'd arrived at—entirely too soon for her liking. While she'd sorted her dirty clothing downstairs, away from Max and his magnetism, she couldn't help but consider how he'd come in and turned her life completely upside down in only three days. All she thought about was Max. All she wanted was Max. While she'd measured out the detergent and sprinkled white powder into the running water, she'd actually imagined what it would be like to live with him in his Russian Hill home. To wake up with him as she had at the guest house this morning, rousing him with soft kisses that led to lazy, wonderful sex. She thought about redecorating his ice-cold living room in Oriental style, merging their homes, merging their lives.

And not once—*not once*—did she think about the restaurant, her long hours, her dream. All of a sudden, her personal goals seemed silly, unimportant and self-ish next to the possibility of love. But hadn't she felt *exactly* the same way with Rick?

Max was not Rick, she knew that with the same certainty that she knew she was no longer the inno-cent child who'd married her first lover for all the wrong reasons. She was older, wiser. And unfortunately, that wisdom included the knowledge that when the week ended and she severed her affair with Max, she was probably letting go of the best thing that had ever happened to her.

"I'm going to go put my stuff in the dryer," she announced, hoping her voice didn't squeak with the sound of tears she could feel coming.

"Need help?" he asked.

She shook her head and pasted on a smile. "No, I can handle it on my own."

She scurried to the door. Laundry, she could do by herself. But the rest of her life? Only three days ago she'd thought she could manage. Now she wasn't so sure.

13

SHE'D BEEN GONE WAY too long. After watching more
of the movie and then realizing he didn't even know
the characters' names, Max had flipped off the television and ventured downstairs. He had no idea where
Mrs. Li's laundry room was, but the hissing rush of
water filling the washing machine drew him in the
right direction.

The intimate space, little larger than a closet, was
tucked in the farthest corner behind the tea shop. A
fluorescent light flickered slightly, casting a harsh
lavender glow over Ariana as she draped damp delicates over the edges of a laundry basket. The curtain
of a tiny window, high in the outer wall, fluttered with
a cool breeze.

She worked mechanically, her gaze glossy and
seemingly unfocused. But from the crease in her forehead and the decided dip of the corners of her mouth,
Max judged he was the cause of her contemplative
expression. He couldn't blame her. He'd allowed his
somber mood to ruin the movie, perhaps the entire
evening. He decided enough was enough. If he
wanted Ariana to seriously consider extending their
relationship beyond the end of the week, he'd better
change tactics quickly.

Impulsively, he flicked off the light switch.

"Hey!" she protested, twirling toward him.

He stepped in immediately, closing and locking the sliding pocket door behind him. ''It's just me,'' he reassured her.

Clutching a pair of bright red panties in her hands, she sighed. Light from the alley flashed in from the high window whenever the wind threw the curtains aside, revealing her relieved expression. ''I'm sorry I'm taking so long. I was just…thinking.''

He took one step closer. ''About us?''

The room wasn't large enough to allow her much of a retreat. When the washing machine stopped her from backing up farther, he moved in and pressed full against her. In an instant, he was hard with wanting. But sex wouldn't be enough this time. Not for him. And he hoped she too was tiring of the game of ''physical pleasure only'' they both were pretending to play. Truth was, in three short days, they'd built the foundation of a relationship that could either be strengthened by honest emotion or would crumble into nothing from too much hesitancy, too much emotional denial.

They both had decisions to make. And he figured there was no time like the present to begin the process.

''What's to think about with us?'' she said flippantly, obviously trying to hide the flustered quiver in her voice with a shrug and a smile. She slipped her arms around his waist and moved to snuggle closer.

He stopped her with a halting grip on her elbows.

''There's a lot to think about, Ariana. A lot to say. You need me to go first? I will.''

Her eyes flashed with a fiery mixture of vexation and bravado. She tried to pull away, but he held her firm. She didn't struggle, just lifted her chin higher. "I'm not afraid of you, Max."

"Of course you aren't. You're afraid of repeating the mistake from your past."

"What is that supposed to mean?"

He paused, tilting his head to the side to tell her silently that he didn't buy her sudden ignorance one iota. But to her credit, she didn't back down. She countered his expression with an impatient huff of her own.

Max softened the tone of his voice. "It's supposed to mean that you have a very clear, very defined mission in life—a mission you've already detoured from once with Rick. And here I am offering another side trip."

"Just for a week. And, for the record, I asked you."

"Yes, *you* asked for just the week. Now I'm asking for more." He released her elbows by sliding his palms down her bare arms, twining his fingers with hers and then lifting their clutched hands to his lips. "You fascinate me, Ari. I've never felt so alive." He skimmed his mouth over her knuckles, then tucked her hands beneath his chin. "I can pinpoint, to the minute, the very moment I realized that I couldn't be poor for the rest of my life. I've devoted my life to attaining wealth. And I missed so much in the process."

Her gaze softened. She slipped her hands from his grasp, caressing his cheeks to soften the blow of her words. "But now you have your success, don't you? You have what you wanted. It's easy to change the direction in your life after if you've reached your destination."

He fought to ignore the lulling sensation of her warm palms on his face. Her point was valid and difficult to dispute. But he had to find a way, or he'd lose her for sure. "I wish it was that easy. You're making me realize that money isn't all I've wanted, Ari. Money was just the easiest thing to attain."

She shook her head. "Easy? Don't you think that's an oversimplification? You've worked hard, Max, sacrificed so much."

He shrugged, knowing he'd busted his butt to attain all he had, giving up a normal childhood and countless social interactions in the process. Until Ari came along, he'd convinced himself that his single-minded focus had been admirable. Requisite. It had given him an edge over other entrepreneurs and upstarts. And until Ari slipped into his life—his heart—he'd believed he had much more to accomplish. Yes, he had wealth, but he still considered himself just a poor kid from Oakland who had somehow managed to do well for himself. He'd been lucky. Knew the right people. Right place, right time.

The Pier deal would win him the unqualified self-respect and security he'd truly desired. He wasn't just making money for himself this time, but for the powerbrokers of San Francisco as well. He was creating a playground for them, with their input as investors. And though the scandal with Ariana could cost him that ultimate triumph, right this very minute he simply didn't care.

He searched the depths of her dark gaze, not speaking until he was sure she was listening. With her heart. With her soul. "And I'm going to continue to work hard until I get *everything* I want. It's just that now I want you too."

Ari sighed, then slipped beneath his arm, darting toward the large washbasin just below the window. She turned the faucets and splashed her face, drawing the moisture through her hair with her wet hands, splattering water across her neck. She sighed again as the cool drops from the tap ran over her skin, though this time the sound resembled more of a coo than an echo of frustration.

Max watched, enthralled, as the droplets kissed her skin. The running dryer infused the air with humid heat, making his breathing even more difficult when Ari shut off the faucet and slowly turned. Glistening, the water dropped off her eyelashes, flowed down her cheeks, throat, breasts.

"You want me? Then have me, Max."

She tucked her hands in the back of her leggings, just enough to stretch open the top of her oversized shirt. She'd left several buttons unfastened so that her thin silvery bra, now spotted and translucent with water, showed him hard evidence of her desire.

"It's hot in here, but we *can* make it hotter," she promised.

Max groaned. "You're trying to distract me."

And her trick was working like a charm. But even her powerful sexuality couldn't overpower his desire to turn their affair in the direction of something more serious, more permanent. As she closed in, she unbuttoned her shirt completely, allowing him to see precisely where the water had drizzled down, over and through her bra. She pushed her shirt off her shoulders, then pressed him backward until the hot metal casing of the dryer warmed through the denim of his jeans.

"Looks that way." She drew her fingers down her

chest, her touch manipulating the moisture on her skin, manipulating him just the same. "I'm all wet." She gripped the dryer on either side of him, trapping him in a box of pure heat. "Maybe we can put this appliance to better use."

God, he couldn't resist her. Not when she moistened her lips so slowly. Not when she slipped her hot, wet hands beneath his shirt and up his chest. He whipped his shirt off in time for her to capture his nipples in her mouth. Moisture and heat assailed him from all angles. She kissed and plucked and bit until the oxygen in his lungs thickened into molten need. She unzipped his jeans and guided him out of them, stripping away his boxers in the process, leaving him naked. He hissed when she pushed him back against the dryer, bare flesh to increasingly hot metal. Her devilish grin heightened the thrill.

She thought she'd conceived the perfect means to keep them from talking further, but Max had learned several important things about Ariana in the past few days. One of them was that she was a woman of action. To tell her he cared for her was one thing. Rick had told her, her parents had told her...and then they'd let her down.

To convince Ariana that he was different, he'd need to show her. And he'd use their intense physical attraction as his medium.

"Too hot for you?" she asked, challenge lilting her voice and lighting her dark eyes.

"With you? Never." He snagged a towel from her laundry basket and spread it on top of the dryer. Bracing his hands on either side, he lifted himself up, breathing out loudly as the heat rumbled beneath him. She wanted to have sex? Fine with him. But he'd turn this into a lesson in trust and sacrifice she wouldn't forget.

Hurriedly, he snared her bra strap with one finger and tugged her between his thighs. "But if you don't hurry up, some very important parts of me—two parts to be exact—might get scorched."

"Aw," she said with an exaggerated pout, cupping and kneading him softly, melding the heat from the dryer with a warmth all her own. "I wouldn't want that to happen."

She pushed his knees farther apart with her other hand and then brazenly cooled his hard sex with a wicked lick, followed by a breathy whistle. The contrast of temperatures—fire beneath him, humidity around him, the chill from the fluttering wind from the window and the gentle warmth of her mouth—clashed into a perfect storm of pleasure.

When she took him completely into her mouth, the tempest raged. He gripped the dryer, then grasped her shoulders, branding her with the heat of his hands, making her gasp even as she brought him nearer and nearer to the edge.

"Ariana, no. Ari, I'm…"

His restraint was tentative, and some of it slipped before he could push her away. He wondered then who was teaching what to whom. She wouldn't move, wouldn't stop loving him until she claimed the prize she wanted. Stubborn as she was giving, she took all he offered, then caressed him back to earth.

He made a move to slide off the dryer, but she stopped him with her palm on his belly. "Let me."

She snatched a condom from the pocket of his discarded jeans, the precise place he'd promised her he'd keep protection during the duration of their affair. She tore open the packet then set it on the washer. With little fanfare, she ripped away her bra, leggings and panties, upended the wicker basket and climbed onto his lap.

With the towel safely beneath him, he scooted back to give them more room, capturing her breast in his mouth, loving the feel of her hardening nipple against the softness of his tongue. The gentle reverberation of the laundry spinning below them thrummed straight through his flesh, coupling with the feel of her wrapping her legs around him until he was quickly aroused again. She slipped the prophylactic on in one quick tug, then moved to help him inside.

She wanted the passion quick. The act fast and frantic and ultimately meaningless. No time to allow the sexual connection to reach her heart. No time for the depth of his passion to touch her soul.

Maybe that's how they'd made love the first night—the night he couldn't remember. But since then their loving had become slower, more attentive, mirroring what he knew was scaring her most.

"Slow down, sweetheart. It's not often I have a beautiful woman straddling me on a dryer. I want to enjoy this."

She bathed his face in a splash of insistent kisses. "Someone could come in and find us."

He stopped her passionate assault by bracing her cheeks in his hands. "No one is going to find us here. It's two o'clock in the morning, the doors are all locked and that window is too small and high for any photographer to peep through." With his thumbs, he stroked from her cheekbones to her lips, skimming her moist mouth, savoring the eroticism of the simple touch. "It's just you and me."

So he took his time, placing sweet, butterfly kisses just above her eyelids, on the tip of her nose, at the lobes of each ear. He stretched her arms across his shoulders, where she laced them behind his neck. Holding her bottom with splayed hands, he kissed a path from her collarbones to her breasts, alternating his mouth from one nipple to the other while his fingers teased and tormented her down below.

"Max, you're killing me," she murmured, only half teasing as he licked a luscious path back to her mouth. He claimed her lips with ravenous want, pulling her closer so he could feel the slick throbbing of her need against his.

"Then we'll both die happy, sweetheart."

God, he wanted to be inside her. Here, now, forever. Blood raged in his ears, louder and hotter than the roll and tumble of the dryer beneath them. Still, he waited, focusing on the textures and tastes of her mouth and skin, biding his time just a minute longer.

She lifted herself and forced the tip of his sex against her, grinning as she realized that unless he moved, her position allowed her ultimate control. He witnessed the flash of power that lit her eyes, the curl of triumph that turned her pouting mouth into a grin.

Sliding one hand between them, she held him stiff against her, both of them breathing in sharply as the sensations rushed and spiked.

"You can have me right now," he told her, making clear the conclusion he needed her to see. Holding out hadn't been easy, but he trusted her to follow his clues to this sweet resolution. "You can have me whenever you want me, Ariana. Wherever. Tonight." He shifted, just enough to slide ever-so-slightly inside her. "Tomorrow." He drew her knees up so her feet were flat against the dryer's control panel, giving her all the leverage, allowing her utter power over their coupling. Utter power over him. "Anytime you want me, I'll be right here."

When he looked up, he knew she understood. Her pupils swelled completely into her irises; her lashes fluttered, polishing her ebony eyes glossy and glossier. Her bottom lip quivered. He hungered to alleviate the shiver with his mouth on hers, but instead he pressed a single kiss on her cheek, drawing his lips upward so he could whisper in his ear.

"Think you can handle all that power?"

With a narrow-eyed gleam that combined determination with desire, he eased inside her. She urged him to thrust and touch her with hot, demanding cries—thrusting and touching him with equal abandon. Hands reached and grasped. Lips clashed. Tongues mated. In a wild instant, they crossed over the edge, her first, then him.

And yet, when the insanity ebbed, Ariana hardly moved. Cradling her cheek on his shoulder, she crossed her legs behind him, drawing her completely against him. He drew his knees up, balancing his feet on the dryer's edge, to brace her back, completing the intimate ball of bodies they formed. And for a long while they sat there, quietly cradled, until a sharp bell signaled the end of the cycle.

ARIANA SNUGGLED INTO the warm sheets on her bed and breathed in the nearly overpowering scent of fresh fabric softener. Without opening her eyes, she grinned. Max didn't know a damn thing about laundry, but he made up for his heavy hand with the Downy by doing delightful deeds with the warmed pillowcases and towels. Yet, as she turned and allowed the morning light to assail her eyes, she remembered the significance that Max's soft ministrations had held. He hadn't just made love with her last night in the euphemistic sense. He'd shown her his love. Lived it. Without the words, yes—he was sharp enough to know that such a declaration would send her running—but he felt the emotion just the same. He'd opened his heart and shown her the contents, forcing her to look inside herself and gauge the depth of her feelings.

And in the bright morning light, she didn't like the results one bit.

She shook her head as she checked the clock at her bedside. Nearly eleven. She groaned, trying to remember when she'd last allowed herself the luxury of sleeping past eight o'clock, even on a rare day off. But Max wore her out. And she'd enjoyed every minute of it. She knew without a doubt that she could sneak back under the covers and fall instantly asleep.

But at eleven o'clock, the morning papers had been on the stands for nearly half a day. She decided to focus on Max's potential trouble with his investors and his Pier deal rather than on her feelings for Max. She would leave that minefield for another time.

She didn't want to love him, dammit. But as she threw on her favorite pink robe, she had a hard time ignoring the cut-and-dried fact that she most probably already did.

The scent of hot coffee wafted from the kitchen and she found Max there, a barely touched mug chilling in front of him. He looked up from *The Bay Area Insider* spread out on the countertop. The rage in his eyes answered her question.

"How bad?" she asked simply. She reached for his cup and found it stone cold. He'd been staring at the paper for a long, long time.

"I called my attorney."

"That bad?" She shot toward the paper, but he stopped her by standing and bracing her shoulders with his hands.

"I..."

She jabbed a finger into his chest, hoping a good fight would alleviate the nauseating pit of dread rolling in her stomach. "Don't apologize again, Max. Just let me see."

He shook his head. "You don't need—"

She exhaled. "Don't tell me what I need and don't need, Max Forrester. You're my lover, not my protector. It's me they got this time, isn't it? You think I'm not going to see it? You think my not seeing it is going to change anything? You called your attorney, for God's sake. Now give me the paper."

In the seconds it took for him to turn around and retrieve the offending page and hand it to her, none of the horrific images that flashed through her mind were as shocking as the actual photograph.

This one wasn't grainy. The black-and-white reproduction was crisp and clear. Her, sitting on the windowsill, rapture overwhelming her features, a man's hands—Max's hands—braced on her knees.

She couldn't read the caption. Her eyes wouldn't focus. The paper fluttered from her fingers. Her stomach clenched into a tight stone and her lungs seemed to reject the small amount of air she managed to pull inside.

"Ariana—" Max reached for her, but she stepped out of range, out of the kitchen. In the living room, her gaze darted to the window. She marched over and flung the curtains aside, nearly tearing the material from the rods. When she spun back around, Max stood at the threshold, his hands clenched in fists within his pockets.

"That picture was taken from across the street."

He nodded. "I know. I visited there this morning. For two hundred dollars, Ty Wong gave me the name of the man who paid him exactly the same amount to let him use his window—a kid with a telephoto lens."

She tugged in some air to control the rage boiling inside her. "Who?"

He shook his head, as if the name was insignificant. "Some guy he knows from rave parties. Leo. Red hair. Three lightning-bolt earrings in his left ear. He didn't know his last…"

"Leo?" She couldn't believe this was happening, but the description had been too precise to be anyone but the Leo she knew. "Leo Glass? Leo did this to me?"

"You know him?"

She stalked across the room, pushing past him in her search for the phone. "I should. I sign his damn paychecks." She found the handset and dug her address book out from behind her cookie jar. She flipped to the G listings and was about to punch in Leo's number when Max stopped her.

"Wait. I don't understand."

"Leo is my backup bartender. One of the guys who covers for me when I'm out or in the kitchen or working the dining room."

"How long has he worked for you?"

Ariana shook her head, attempting to reach beyond her anger long enough to answer Max's question. She knew she had to act rationally, think about this and work through the hows and whys. But, dammit, right now all she wanted to do was kick that scrawny son of a bitch in his cocky little ass.

"I hired him, I don't know, six months ago."

"He's a good employee?"

She shrugged. He wasn't the best on her staff. He tended to flirt too much with the young female tourists, bucking for bigger tips. Hell, he'd flirted with her one time too many until she'd finally set him straight.

"Was he working Friday night?" Max asked. The struggle on his face, his intense focus on putting this puzzle together into a logical explanation snapped her back to reality. Until they understood, they couldn't protect themselves, couldn't strike back with accuracy. Her anger would have to wait, just until she told Max what he needed to know.

"Yeah. He was tending bar when I got there."

"So he could have slipped that drug in my beer."

Ariana nodded. And if Ty Wong knew Leo Glass from raves—the late-night, techno-music parties where drugs usually flowed more readily than even alcohol— he had access to whatever had been put into Max's drink.

"Easily. But why? What does he have against you?"

Max shook his head. "You're his boss. What does he have against you?"

The question stunned them both to silence. Leo Glass was somehow connected to both of them, though even from Ty's description, Max could barely remember what he looked like. Now that he knew the punk worked for Ariana, he did vaguely remember the carrottop kid. When Max frequented Athens by the Bay, he usually sat on the outside terrace. In the early mornings, Ray, the manager, usually waited tables. In the evenings, an older waiter named Johnny and his wife—the crusty, but lovable Aida—covered the outdoor crowd. If he'd somehow managed to piss off this Leo fellow, he couldn't imagine how or when. The punk had to have taken the photographs for money—money from someone trying to sabotage Max's life. That he was a regular in Ari's restaurant made him an easy target of Leo's watchful eye. But why would he put Ari in the middle? Why embarrass her? She'd been identified in this caption, along with the restaurant's name and location. Unless she had simply been at the wrong place—with him—at the wrong time.

"Maybe you should get dressed," Max suggested, attempting to pull the address book and phone out of her hand. "We need to sort this out. Figure out this kid's motive. His connection to both of us."

Her nod was nearly imperceptible, but she released the book and phone and disappeared into her bedroom without another word. Max was scanning the open page for the kid's listing when the phone trilled in his hand.

He answered immediately. "Karas residence."

"Max, you gotta get down here!" ever-relaxed, ever-laid-back Charlie barked into the phone.

"I can't...I have—"

"Max, trust me. Whatever is going on there is nothing compared to the crap happening here."

14

AFTER HAILING A CAB to his house to change clothes, Max drove to the office, parked and walked through a gauntlet of screaming reporters who had staked out his reserved spot. Shouting "No comment" as he strode to the bank of elevators to the twenty-fourth floor, he ducked out of the light of the cameras and wondered if these vultures had found Ariana.

Reluctantly, he'd left without her, but she'd out and out told him that she needed time to deal with this alone—to find Leo so he could be dealt with. Max highly suspected that a plan of retribution was forming in that incredibly sharp brain of hers, but he didn't ask for details. He'd asked her to wait for his return before she did anything and had elicited a tentative agreement. He forced his focus to quelling the catastrophe Charlie had screamed about on the phone.

The reception area of Forrester Properties was eerily quiet. The young girl who took care of the phones and greeted clients was suspiciously absent from her post. Max fought a growl as he made his way through the maze of cubicles and offices his agents used. Those on the phone were talking in hushed whispers. The rest gathered in groups of two and three, talking frantically until they saw him. Then silence thundered in his ears. Charlie, waiting for him in his office, effectively undid the quiet with his instantaneous, frenetic shouting.

"Randolph and his core investors have been calling all morning." Charlie slammed the door behind him. "Aunt Barbara showed up, bawling her eyes out, wondering where the hell her daughter is, wondering how she'll deal with the humiliation of having her daughter dumped by a philandering cheat. What am I supposed to tell them?"

Max took a deep breath and poured a cup of coffee from the carafe behind his desk. He nodded, trying to remain cool, trying to center on something simple—like how impressed he was that his secretary filled the thermos when he was supposed to be on vacation. He took a sip, slightly disappointed that she hadn't laced the drink with something stronger than cream and sugar.

"Don't tell them anything," Max answered once the heat of the coffee dissolved the baseball-size pit in his stomach. "I'll handle this."

"You're back in the game? For good?"

Max shook his head. Now that Ariana had been pulled into his mess, or he into hers—he wasn't sure which since they both had been targeted by the same jerk with a camera—he had no intention of leaving her to deal with the backlash alone. "I'm here now for damage control. But I'm out of here by tonight. Ariana and I have a photographer to find."

"Where is she now?"

Max shrugged and fell into his leather wingback chair. "She said she was going to find her uncle."

"You don't believe her?"

"Ariana has a mind and a will of her own. I called my brother and asked him to keep her company, but she was already gone by the time he arrived at her apartment.''

For now, he'd give her the space she needed and handle things from his end.

"First order of business," Max directed, snatching a pen from a leather-trimmed cup and jotting notes as he spoke. "Find Madelyn for Barbara. Your aunt doesn't deserve to be worried. I assume you told her that Madelyn is fine, that *she* chose to run away on her own?"

Charlie nodded. "I told her. I also put a call in to Maddie's cell phone. She'll check in when she gets the message. She never intended her quest for independence to hurt anyone, least of all her parents. She lied about the elopement to save face for them, not for herself. She thought a week of downtime would lessen the blow."

"Maddie didn't know *The Bay Area Insider* was going to get involved. What about the Darlington Group?"

Charlie tugged a chair closer to Max's desk and fell into the stiff cushions. "Ambrose wants us to meet as soon as possible. He doesn't give a shit what you do with your private life, but his brother isn't so liberal or forgiving."

As if Max needed anyone's forgiveness for finding the woman of his dreams. But he put aside his comments, just as he'd put aside his emotions, for the time being. Max had become adept at suppressing his feelings to focus on business. He'd always considered that a talent until Ariana pulled it on him this morning. Urging him to the office had been an effective means of keeping her heart safe for another day. But the sooner he handled this crisis, the sooner he could find her.

"Bottom line?" Max asked.

Charlie leaned back and stared at the ceiling. "They don't want any more controversy associated with this project. They came to San Francisco to live, Max. They want to be perceived as part of the community, not 'heartless interlopers who shanghaied a historical landmark for commercial rape.'"

Charlie quoted a line from *The Bay Area Insider*'s latest editorial with clear disdain. He and Max both knew that the paper's opinion was crap. Pure bleeding-heart, antidevelopment crap. Worst part was, through the course of this deal Max hadn't had a clear enemy on whom to blame the propaganda. Not one neighborhood or civic group had formed to fight the development. Not one individual had come out as a leader in the opposition. He'd been fighting the phantom "general public" as reported in the news—until now.

He dug into his briefcase and extracted the offending newspaper, turning to the masthead to read the name of the editor. Donalise Parker. Never heard of her. The reporters who'd covered the deal in the past and who'd interviewed him for the slanted stories they'd printed had each been different. All young, all hungry, and not one with the savvy or experience to orchestrate the level of hostility he'd been contending with.

But printing a photograph of Ariana rated as an act of war, especially when the caption left no question as to her identity. They'd not only printed her name and the location of her business, they'd implied that she was the reason for Saturday's canceled Forrester-

Burrows wedding. Though written tongue in cheek, the commentary thanked Ariana for breaking up not only a marriage but also one of the "most offensive real estate transactions the city has ever faced."

He swallowed his rage with another sip of coffee, forcing himself to tear the editor's name out of the paper without ripping the newsprint to shreds. He handed the jagged scrap to Charlie. "Call the Darlingtons and your uncle Randolph and set up a meeting for three o'clock. Then call this Donalise Parker and tell her I'd like to speak with her. Right away."

Charlie scanned the clipping. "You're going to talk to the newspaper editor? Why not the owner?"

Max grabbed his phone to dial his lawyer again. He wasn't going to march into the offices of *The Bay Area Insider* with a full patrol from Gonzalez, Oehler and Powell, Attorneys-at-Law, in tow. He'd handle this himself. However, he wasn't foolish enough to confront the press without a strong dose of legal advice.

"Because the owner is some European conglomerate just making the move into media." A few phone calls on the way over had netted him that knowledge. "They dole out the cash, but they don't mess with the content. I've got to find out where this opposition is coming from...why they're stooping to personal assassination in order to stop us dead. The Pier was a rotting pile of smelly, barnacle-encrusted wood that no one cared about until we came in with a plan not only to make some money, but bring more people to that area of the Wharf. Until today, I thought *The Bay Area Insider* was just stirring up trouble for the sake of stirring up trouble, like the media often does. Now I'm not so sure."

"You think they have another agenda?"

Max flashed him the picture of Ariana, briefly, before folding the newsprint into a tight rectangle, photo-side down.

"Go make those phone calls. I want to check in with Ari."

Charlie rose and walked toward the door, his shoulders slumped and his gait sluggish. He turned before he grabbed the doorknob, wincing as if he finally realized the price this mess was costing Max's lover. "How is she holding up? She's gotta be humiliated."

With Charlie well across the room, Max felt safe to turn the newspaper over and run his hand over the offending picture—even though his friend and a majority of San Francisco had already seen and dissected the photo *The Bay Area Insider* chose to print. Though snapped in profile, Max could easily superimpose the other side of her face from memory. Her eyes had been closed. Her mouth open, lips shaped in a delicate O. The breeze fluttered her hair, tangling the dark strands with the ruby curtains, creating an image he suddenly realized was incredibly aesthetic. Her beauty—exotic, wild—belonged in a gallery...to be admired, not disdained.

She didn't deserve this. And he wondered if he deserved her.

"She's angry. Furious. The guy who took this picture works for her."

Charlie stalked back to Max's desk, his whisper echoing his shock. "At the restaurant?"

Staring, Max conveyed the implications of this too-coincidental-to-be-a-coincidence turn. He wasn't a big fan of conspiracy theories, but he couldn't ignore the facts. He and Ariana had become an item, he thought, purely by chance. Leo Glass was either a brilliant mastermind or the luckiest son of a bitch in San Francisco.

"Yeah, and right now, he's M-I-A. As soon as I've taken care of the Darlingtons and the investors, we're going to look for him and find out who he's really working for."

Charlie's face skewed with skepticism. "You sure Ariana isn't already looking without you?"

Max shook his head, denying himself the frightening images that scenario presented. "No, I'm not sure. I'm not sure of a lot of things. But I intend to be—very soon."

ARIANA STRETCHED HER NECK from side to side, then in one full rotation winced as kinks and cricks popped from her vertebrae. It had been a long morning. A long, fruitless morning. Leo Glass had apparently disappeared off the face of the earth. She had a good idea where he'd surface next, delaying her retribution until late tonight. Waiting, doing nothing, wasn't an option she preferred. Doing nothing meant she had to think, and her thoughts ultimately drifted to Max.

"Here, drink this."

Her uncle poured a shot glass of crisp, clear ouzo and slid it toward her. His lined face and tanned, stubbled jowls bore none of his usual good humor this morning. Even before Ariana sneaked in through the restaurant's back door, eluding the reporter who'd staked out the front entrance, he'd seen the photo that had the Wharf in an uproar. She could only imagine what comments and crudities his cronies had tortured him with. By the time she'd arrived, he'd dismissed the crew that had been dismantling and storing equipment in preparation of the upcoming construction.

It was just the two of them. And though Ariana normally didn't imbibe alcohol before the evening hours, she did as he ordered and swallowed the liqueur in one quick gulp.

He let her regain her breath before he posed his first question.

"Do you love this man?" Stefano asked.

That wasn't the question she expected.

She tipped the empty glass over her lips again, hoping a dash more ouzo would help. "I've only known him—really known him—for a few days."

Stefano's expression portrayed his disbelief. "Ari, time doesn't matter. You married your first husband after knowing him less than that."

She nodded. "And we know how that turned out."

His expression was incredulous. "Rick may not have deserved your love, but that didn't change how you felt about him. I'm not asking you if this affair with Max Forrester is going to last beyond next week. I'm asking if you love him."

Ariana toyed with the empty shot glass, twirling her finger around the smooth lip, recalling with crystal clarity how she'd done the same to the glass she'd served Max's Flaming Eros in just before she touched him for the first time.

"I can't fall in love with him. Look around us!" She gestured to the near-empty room that had once been a cluttered, vibrant bar. The mirrored shelves behind her uncle were almost completely bare. The tables and chairs and bar stools, save one or two, had been dragged away and stacked in a moving trailer parked around back. "We're about to dive into some serious debt here. I can't—*we* can't—afford to be distracted now."

He nodded as he cleared away her glass, but she could tell he wasn't buying her argument. He came out from behind the bar and dragged a battered stool beside hers, taking her hand in his as he sat. "Love is the ultimate distraction, isn't it? But you know I loved your aunt with all my heart. From the instant I set eyes on her, I didn't want anything else but to make love to her…all the time. That was 1955," he clarified with a pointed finger on the bar.

"Is that why you married her so quickly?"

He chuckled, flipping off his battered captain's hat, then setting it back down at an angle that looked rakish and dashing, even though he was long beyond seventy and had put on a good sixty pounds of extra weight. But until the day she died, Sonia Karas had watched her husband with adoring eyes. Ariana had seen their love for herself. She imagined that her aunt Sonia hadn't stood a chance of escaping this man's charm.

"Three days we knew each other." He rolled his eyes heavenward as he recalled the tempest of their whirlwind romance. "Her father would have hung me from his largest fish hook if I hadn't produced that marriage license."

Ariana laughed with him. They both knew the stories, knew the history of the forty-five year marriage during which Stefano and Sonia had worked together side by side, all day, every day. They'd had their arguments—loud ones, passionate ones—but they'd never tired of each other, never lost that spark of respect and desire that even strangers could see. They'd never even spent a night apart—not since their wedding on the run from Sonia's father and half-dozen brothers.

For a while, Ariana had hoped she'd find something similar with Rick—something exciting and forbidden and wild. They'd had the desire but never the respect.

And with Max? Even in the face of horrible humiliation, Ariana still considered him a remarkable man, full of integrity. Honor. His instinct to protect and avenge her was strong, and yet he managed— only at her request—to rein in his natural inclination to find Leo himself and beat the living daylights out of him. By simply trusting her to find Leo herself, respecting her need to retain some semblance of control, he'd shown her once again that he was more than worthy of her love.

"So? Do you love him?"

She laid her palm over her uncle's hands, relishing the warmth of his weathered experience. No sense running from the truth any longer, at least not with her uncle. He'd been her only family since she'd come to San Francisco. And after all the grief she'd caused him over the photo, she at least owed him some honesty.

"Yeah, I do. Something fierce. Isn't it awful?"

"Awful? Ari, that's wonderful!"

"How is it wonderful?"

Stefano shook his head. "He's a smart man who worked hard and made good. Don't think I didn't check him out a long time ago, when I first noticed him making goo-goo eyes at you."

Ariana wasn't the least surprised that Stefano would find out all he could about Max. And it wouldn't have been hard since Max came in the restaurant all the time.

"Yeah, well, making a success of himself in this town means a lot to him. He goes to charity functions and all the right parties. I need to be here, where my dream is. A wife should be with her husband."

Stefano snorted. "Yeah, you were with Rick. You used to call the clubs and book his shows before he got a promoter. Used to inventory his equipment. Hell, girl, you used to help lug his speakers in and out of that beat-up van. You were a damn good wife by your definition. Where did it get you?"

"Divorced. Single. Which is maybe where I should be. I have dreams of my own, Stefano. You know that more than anyone. I can't give them up."

"Is he asking you to?"

"Max? No! Of course not. He'd never ask. He just figures we'd find a way to make it work."

Stefano nodded and stood, dragging the stool with him and stashing it in the bare alcove that had once been their hostess station. "You're afraid to fail again, Ari. Afraid to have your heart broken. That's nothing to be ashamed of, but it's also no reason to be stupid. If you love this man, if you believe he loves you, then you're a damn idiot to walk away."

Stefano huffed when he finished his tirade, just to make sure she was paying close attention. Then he waited...for her to agree? Ari sighed, joining Stefano in the alcove after lifting her stool and stacking it atop his. She knew her uncle was right. Knew only a "damn idiot" would let a man like Max go. And even though she'd claimed for years—including the first night they'd made love on his balcony—that a fear of heights was the only thing she was scared of, she knew now she'd been telling Max a big fat lie.

She was afraid of falling in love again. Of getting her heart broken yet again. Of losing herself in a man after she'd fought so hard to gain her independence after her divorce. And she also worried that this fear was one she'd never overcome.

"Stefano, I'm sorry if I embarrassed you with that photograph. We should have been more discreet."

Draping his burly arm over her shoulder, he led her toward the back office. There was work to be done today, and none of it could be completed at the restaurant. "I'm your uncle, not your father. You don't live in San Francisco for fifty-five years without developing some tolerance for unusual behavior. You don't worry about me."

He kissed her on the cheek and she knew the incident was done. "Thank you."

His "you're welcome" was a chesty grunt. "So, do you need any help making this matter right? I know a couple of mean sailors who might be looking for some extra cash."

Ariana laughed, not doubting for a moment that Stefano did indeed know someone she could pay to break Leo Glass's legs—and his camera—for little more than a night's worth of tips. "Thanks, Uncle Stefano. I'll keep that in mind."

He kissed her other cheek, then unlocked the back door and checked in both directions for any sign of trouble, waving her through once he was certain the coast was clear. He pressed a set of keys into her hand. "Take my truck and do what you have to do. Leo doesn't know who he's messing with."

That might be true, but, for that matter, neither did

Max Forrester. But after tonight they'd both know. And maybe she'd know herself. As she skipped over a puddle and ducked around a trash bin to where Stephano parked his truck, Ariana realized that she couldn't deal with Max and his suggestion that they extend their affair until she first dealt with the contents of her own heart.

15

ARIANA'S FIRST INSTINCT was to hold her breath. Pungent smoke, thicker than fog and ripe with marijuana and tobacco, drew the multicolored haze into a sickening swirl. Sweetened by the overpowering mixture of cheap perfumes, colognes and sweat, the air stung her eyes and burned the back of her throat. But she carefully kept a disgusted snort to herself. This world of raves and music wasn't hers, but she needed to exist here long enough to find Leo Glass.

Ty Wong had assured her that Leo would be at this party. And after infiltrating several rave parties and dance clubs all night, she just wanted to find his scrawny, deceitful butt, force the whole truth out of him and leave.

To go back to Max. Back to adulthood. Back to worrying about the contents of her heart rather than the safety of her body.

''There. In the corner.''

Ty pointed toward a shadowed spot far from the front door of the abandoned building the teens and twenty-somethings had commandeered for the rave. Techno-music blared from speakers that probably cost more than her apartment. Girls in barely-there tank tops and hip-hugging capri pants chatted between sucking on pacifiers and drinking bottled water by the gallon. Guys made the rounds, a few hanging tight to helium balloons, some made from inflated condoms. Ty had already explained the uses and reasons for such odd sights, incongruous and childlike. Pacifiers. Balloons. Toys used to play with drugs like Ecstasy, the psychedelic of choice with this partying set.

This wasn't her world, thank God. She preferred her ecstasy to be of the sensual kind. The kind Max gave her rather than some chemical wrapped in a pill.

Ty started to walk away, but she grabbed his arm. "Where do you think you're going?" she asked, delivering her toughest sneer to the reed-thin excuse for a man she'd been forced to take on as her guide.

"I told you I'd help you find Leo Glass. I did that. I'm outta here."

She didn't release him, even when he tugged. "You still want me to ask your uncle *not* to throw you out of your rent-free apartment?"

He stopped struggling. "Hey, man. That was the deal."

"Well, man—" she poked his chest, not surprised to instantly meet the feel of bone through his T-shirt "—then you better get Leo for me and bring him outside. This place stinks. I need air."

Ty hesitated, but nodded. The strands of hair he'd dyed blue swung into his face. Until she got an explanation from Leo Glass, if not his head on a platter, she would manipulate Ty however she could. It had been a long time since Ariana had been this angry. Unfortunately for Leo Glass and Ty Wong and anyone else who got in her way, she was going to settle this score on her own terms.

That's why she'd left without returning Max's half-dozen calls. At the time, she told herself she had to prove to Max that she could take care of herself. He was so powerful, so commanding, so at ease in the world of giving orders and orchestrating events to his advantage. But after the first descent into this foreign social world, she acknowledged that her fear of falling in love had sent her running from Max. She was afraid of trusting again. Loving again.

Once certain Ty was doing as she requested and wasn't trying to sneak out a side door, she made a beeline for the exit. She took a deep, invigorating breath of garbage-scented air outside, thinking it the freshest fragrance she'd inhaled in a long time. She stepped toward the truck she'd borrowed from her uncle, when she heard her name shouted over the residual pounding of music from inside.

She turned, expecting to see Leo. Instead she found Max. She should have realized he'd find her. That he wouldn't let her get away so easily. Her admiration for this man warred with her need to put this matter to rest on her own.

"Max? What are you doing here?"

"Looking for you." He shoved his hands into the pockets of his jeans, rage firing his green eyes and tempered only by the unmistakable softness of relief. "I know you said you needed to find Leo on your own, but...these parties aren't safe. Ford and I have been all over town looking for you. What were you thinking?"

She bit back her anger when his tone altered from concern to condescension. She didn't need Max following her, tracking her down, playing knight in shining armor to her damsel in distress. She'd taken damn good care of herself so far. She didn't need his rescuing. But, God help her, his concern felt like a soft, wool blanket on a wet, cold night.

She pushed the warmth away. "How did you find me?"

Max glanced over his shoulder. Ford, lingering on the sidewalk beside Max's Porsche, waved. "My brother is very good at finding people."

"Yeah, well," she murmured, impressed despite her annoyance. "I should have let you throw him to the sharks when I had the chance."

"Probably." Max chuckled. "Did you find Leo?"

She glanced behind her at the battered steel door of the building, barely lit by the glow of a nearby street lamp. The parking lot was full of cars. At least twenty kids hung out on the weed-infested blacktop, sitting on the hoods, talking and laughing and having a much better time than she was.

"He should be coming out any minute."

Max nodded, then scanned the area as he took Ari's arm and led her into the light. Gazes darted at them from all directions and conversations stopped.

"You look like a cop," she pointed out, gesturing at his clothes. He was dressed casually in faded jeans, a polo shirt and dock shoes, but he still looked out of place in this setting.

"Sorry, my oversized Tommy Hilfiger outfit is at the cleaners."

His attempted joke succeeded. She chuckled, briefly imagining Max in baggy jeans slung low on his hips, boxers peeking out at the waistband beneath a floppy T-shirt and a sideways ball cap. She liked him better in his jogging clothes, or in those sexy, tailored suits. She liked him naked most of all, but now didn't seem the time to admit her preference.

The door behind them opened and Ty emerged. Ariana turned, then sought Max's gaze.

"Please let me handle this, Max. Leo betrayed me most of all."

He hesitated, but then nodded and stepped back into the shadows. Close, but out of sight. Her heart swelled. Max trusted her, even though his own success with the Pier deal could be on the line.

She suddenly felt like a fool. Not because she had absolutely no idea what to say now that Leo was approaching, but because she'd let one minute pass without realizing how much she loved Max Forrester. Yeah, he'd found her when she'd wanted to confront Leo alone, but he was backing away, giving her control, just as he had when they made love. Just as he had since the very beginning, whenever she wanted to take the lead. She'd simply been too afraid to see that, unlike her family, Max trusted her to make good decisions. And, unlike Rick, he didn't need to control her choices in order to elevate his own sense of power.

"Well, if it isn't San Francisco's sexiest home-wrecker," Leo said with a slur, kicking up gravel as he shuffled closer. She defensively held up her hands, palms up. She didn't think Leo would strike her, but she had a strong suspicion he might lose his balance and topple over. Ty slinked back inside.

"Hello, Leo," Ariana greeted, her tone even. Once certain of his balance, she slid her hands into the pockets of her leather blazer. "You're not an easy guy to find."

"Can't say the same, can you?"

She conceded his point with a shrug. "You got me. You got me good. Care to tell me why?"

He rolled his eyes and chortled; his breath nearly knocked her a few steps back, but she held steady.

"Easy money. The old man wanted the inside scoop on that Forrester guy, and he paid cash."

"Old man? What old man?"

"Burrows. The bank guy."

Ariana shrugged. The only Burrows she knew was Charlie, and he was in real estate. Oh, and Maddie.

Wait a minute. Wasn't Maddie's father, Randolph Burrows, the president of First Financial? Ariana glanced over her shoulder at the shadow where she knew Max lingered, where she was certain he could hear every word they spoke. He stepped slightly forward into the light. The rage in his eyes easily bored through the darkness.

She turned back to Leo. "Randolph Burrows put you up to this? Did he say why?"

"Something about his daughter. Something about Forrester cheating on her or some shit. I don't know. I don't remember. I just know I was supposed to get pictures of the guy with some chick, any chick. But the man was a fuckin' monk—until I placed that roofie in his drink, until you came along. You're one hot piece of ass, you know that?''

Ariana clenched her mouth tightly closed, willing her dinner to remain in her stomach and her hands to remain by her sides. ''Yeah, you told me that once, remember. I set you straight about talking trash to me. I don't suppose my lecture had anything to do with this?''

Leo only laughed. ''I saw you watching Forrester all the time. Heard his friend talking about fixing you two up. Pairing you was fuckin' brilliant, don't you think? Brought you both down at the same time.''

''Brilliant,'' she begrudgingly agreed. She'd always suspected Leo Glass was a smarmy type, but so long as he showed up to the restaurant on time, worked his entire shift, got the orders right and was polite to the customers, she'd been a satisfied boss. She'd forgiven his one breach of decorum, ascribing the crude come-on that she barely remembered to a case of youth and hormones.

This time, he'd crossed the line. But she held back her retribution until she had the final piece of the puzzle. ''And the newspaper? Did the old man arrange for the photos to be printed there?''

Leo clucked away her suggestion. ''Hell, no. He wanted to keep the whole thing private. But I'm no idiot. I *do* read. I knew the press was all over Forrester for that thing with the Pier, so after I collected from the old man, I went to see the editor with a second set of prints.''

The hollowness in her chest expanded as more and more anger burbled up from the pit in her stomach.

As Leo had said, it had all been too easy. Ruining her reputation and Max's deal. Well, it was just as simple for her to put a crimp in Leo's future. "I hope you got paid well...since you're now unemployed."

"You can't fire me!"

She tilted an eyebrow, but didn't say another word. She sure as hell could fire him. "Already spent your payoff, didn't you?" she asked.

His glazed eyes betrayed him. Leo was back where he'd started from. Good.

"Doesn't matter," he spat. "I can get another job."

She nodded. "Yeah, you can. However, unless you want me making sure your new boss knows all about this incident, you're going to take us back to your apartment and watch us burn whatever is left of your film."

Max didn't miss the "us" she purposefully placed in her demand. He stepped forward and waved for Ford to join them. Not only wasn't she stupid enough to go anywhere with Leo without protection, she no longer wanted to.

She'd proved her point. To him. To herself.

Being in control, being strong and independent, wasn't all it was cracked up to be. She'd won with Leo, but the victory was somehow hollow without Max at her side.

Leo cursed the minute he saw Max.

Max placed a protective arm over her shoulder and, this time, she allowed the warmth of his concern to flow through her.

"Ari, why don't we let Ford take Leo home for

that little fire party. You and I have someone else we need to see.''

She pushed the button on her watch, her weary eyes widening at the hour. "It's 3:00 a.m., Max. Do you think Maddie's father wants to see us in the middle of the night?''

"I don't much care what Randolph wants at this point." He skimmed his hand down her arm, then back up from wrist to cheek, as Ford led Leo to Max's car. His caress ignited a burning deep within her, incinerating her residual anger at Leo's self-serving actions.

"You handled Leo incredibly well,'' he murmured.

She leaned her face into his palm, reveling in the soothing feel of his skin against hers. Max was a balm more potent than any of Mrs. Li's teas, more intoxicating than the ouzo her uncle served. She wanted nothing more than to take him home and show him, as he'd shown her, that she was more than willing to find some compromise that would make their relationship work beyond the end of the week.

But they had one stop to make first. One last piece of the scandal to put to rest.

THOUGH THE CLOCK in the Porsche read three-thirty, the windows of the Burrows mansion in Nob Hill were ablaze with light. Max hadn't called ahead, preferring the element of surprise to ensure that Randolph told him the entire truth of his involvement with Leo Glass, Donalise Parker and the scandal that had nearly ruined his relationship with Ariana, not to mention the development deal at the Pier.

But Charlie had obviously beaten him to the punch. Max pulled up behind Charlie's car and parked the truck Ariana had borrowed from her uncle. Max hoped his friend was there because he'd heard from Maddie—and that the news was good.

The butler opened the door shortly after Max knocked, not the least ruffled by greeting visitors in his pajamas and robe. He ushered them into the study and offered freshly brewed coffee from a silver serving set.

"Mr. Burrows will be down momentarily," the butler assured them, then left.

Ariana stood in the doorway, surveying the opulence of the house with wary eyes. "So this is what old money looks like."

"Some of the oldest in the city," Max verified while he poured and mixed two cups of strong java for both of them. He handed her a cup and gestured for her to sit. She shook her head, taking her first sip without moving farther into the room.

Max couldn't help but grin. She wove her way through raves and clubs with ease. She handled Leo with conviction and control. But Randolph's wealth gave her pause.

He recalled with all too much clarity the intimidation he'd faced the first time Maddie had brought him to her parents' home. He understood perfectly what Ariana was thinking as her gaze scanned the antique furniture and original artwork. *I don't belong here. I don't fit in.*

"Money is money, new or old," he assured her,

cupping her elbow with his palm and leading her to a leather love seat tucked near the window.

"Leo betrayed me for money."

"The quest for cash can make people do all sorts of stupid things." Since knowing Ariana, he'd honestly begun to see that truth with painful clarity. Most of his stupidity had luckily harmed only himself. He'd missed out on so much—experiences and emotions Ariana had shown him over the past few days. Adventure, risk, desire. Love. But of all the places in the world to admit that to her, inside Randolph's study wouldn't do. They'd put this episode to rest and then move on to what he now knew to be the more important things.

"Do you think that's why Randolph got involved with Leo?" she asked. "For money?"

Max shook his head. That scenario didn't make any sense. The money to be had was with Max and the Pier deal—the deal Max had brought to Randolph's attention nearly a year ago. But without a doubt, Randolph and Leo had nearly ruined everything.

He and Charlie had met with the Darlingtons and the other investors earlier as planned, and performing their best tap dance, had soothed the uproar. Max hadn't had time to worry about why his former father-in-law-to-be had missed the gathering. The meeting had run long and he'd barely made his appointment with Donalise Parker of *The Bay Area Insider*.

"No, but money is the reason *The Bay Area Insider* printed the pictures. Increased circulation, just as we suspected. No big conspiracy there."

"You found Donalise Parker?"

Max downed more coffee. "She wasn't happy meeting me, but her largest advertiser was a client of mine."

And that fact had given him the idea of how to handle the newspaper once and for all.

"And she verified what Leo told us?"

"She paid him for the pictures and wrote the copy herself. Her paper appeals mainly to the young crowd, and she wanted to reach a bigger demographic. The development controversy, the sex scandal with a major player—too much titillation for her readers for her to pass up on."

Ariana set her cup and saucer down on the side table. "Then what's to keep her from sending someone else after us?"

Max grinned, knowing Ariana would enjoy his tale as much as he loved telling it. "I brought along a copy of the classified section of her paper. I carefully pointed out all the real estate agents' ads—all the agents who were friends or acquaintances I could easily persuade to suspend their advertising dollars. Her tabloid stood to lose some serious cash flow."

Ariana clapped her hands on her knees. "You didn't! I love it. But aren't real estate ads tiny? How bad could that really hurt them?"

Charlie entered the room at that moment, shaking his head and chuckling since he knew the rest of the story firsthand. "You should have seen him, Ariana. He saved the big gun for last."

Max shrugged off Charlie's compliment, but pride swelled his chest all the same. Though he wanted to find out what Charlie was doing here at nearly four

in the morning looking as if he'd been here for a l[...]
while, he chose to finish telling Ariana this story firs[...]
Easing her mind took precedence over everything
else. *She* took precedence over everything else.

"The investors I organized for the Pier deal run the
gamut of the financial world," he explained. "Bankers like Randolph. CEOs of major corporations. Bro-
kers. I just showed Ms. Parker a letter we'd hashed
out at our meeting that promised to cancel approxi-
mately fifty percent of her entire advertising revenue
if she didn't cease and desist her personal attacks."

"We should have thought of it the first time they
complained about the Pier deal," Charlie groused as
he poured coffee for himself.

Max clucked his tongue. "Now, Charles. That
wouldn't be fair. Silencing the press, denying their
First Amendment rights with blatant blackmail."

His holier-than-thou tone didn't fool Ari one bit.
"Isn't that what you did anyway?"

Max set his coffee down and then did the same to
hers. "As far as I'm concerned, Donalise Parker for-
feited those rights when she printed that picture of
you." He took her hands in his, massaging her fingers. He realized then that he couldn't stand being
near her and not touch her. No matter what happened
in the next few days, he couldn't possibly let her go.

"Luckily, Ms. Parker agreed to my terms. And as
soon as we find out what Randolph had to do with
all this…"

Randolph stormed into the study at the sound of
his name. "…You can go back to having your sordid
little affair with impunity." His voice brimmed with

tightly controlled annoyance, softened only by the pure exhaustion that reddened his eyes.

Max stood, taking Ariana's hand as she rose beside him. "Watch what you say, Randolph," Max warned. His tone was even, but the threat was clear. "The one who made our affair sordid was you."

Randolph stopped, dead still, and Ariana watched as the two men squared off and psychologically and physically took their corners. Randolph strolled to the other side of his desk. Max pulled her with him and then offered her a seat directly across from the massive antique table. Ariana didn't want to sit, but when Max silently insisted by turning the chair toward her, she didn't argue.

He remained standing, as did Randolph. Charlie stayed at the sideboard, idly stirring his coffee, which Ariana knew for a fact he drank black and with no sugar.

"I want you off the Pier deal," Randolph demanded, slamming his fist on the leather blotter.

Charlie's eyebrows rose over wide eyes.

Max hooked his thumbs on his belt loops.

"It's my deal, Randolph. I personally recruited every single investor, including you. Why would I back off now, when I stand to make millions? Was that your scheme? To force me out?"

Ariana watched Randolph fume at Max's confidence, his easy, level tone and utter disregard for the older man's command. Randolph's nostrils flared like a raging bull's, but he folded himself into his chair, gripping the armrests. "You've humiliated my daughter, my family."

"I would never do anything to hurt Madelyn," Max said evenly.

Randolph growled. "You didn't love her!" he insisted. "And you were going to marry her anyway. For her money. Her position."

Max took that moment to sit. He couldn't argue that point with Randolph, Ariana knew. But Max did care for Madelyn and, in many ways, Ariana was grateful. His caring for his friend, no matter how selfishly motivated in the beginning, had played a hand in bringing Max and Ariana together. Knowing that talking about his feelings for Maddie would be difficult for him with her there, she laid her hand over his and gave his knuckles a little squeeze.

He rewarded her with a tilted, grateful grin. "I loved Maddie enough to try and make her happy. She only wanted to marry me to please you and Barbara. But she came to her senses and changed her mind. She didn't want to jeopardize the Pier deal by canceling the wedding, so she pulled a disappearing act and asked me to lie low until she could tell you the truth herself. Obviously, you found out sooner, thanks to Leo Glass."

Randolph winced at the mention of Leo's name. "Did he tell you how he broke our deal by selling the photographs to the newspaper? The humiliation Barbara has faced! Both of us! This is exactly what I suspected would happen." He wagged his finger. "I knew your uncouth ways would come back to denigrate this family. I only wish Madelyn had come to her senses sooner."

Max swallowed whatever bitterness Randolph's

reference to his past caused. "Why didn't you warn her about me before? We were engaged for six months."

"I encouraged Madelyn's relationship with you because of Barbara. For whatever reason, my wife likes you. I couldn't openly oppose you without proof of your coarse character."

"So you hired Leo Glass."

"I hired a private investigator. Your business dealings were all legitimate, but you spent an inordinate amount of time at Ms. Karas's restaurant. Mr. Glass pointed us in the direction of your affair."

Ariana had remained silent long enough. "What affair? Max and I had never even been alone together until Friday night."

"Yes, my dear." Randolph said with a condescending nod. "You slept with the groom on the night before his wedding. How genteel of you."

She started to stand and protest, but Max stilled her with one glance. A glance that said, "Let me." He'd deferred the Leo situation to her. Fairness dictated she give him the same consideration with Randolph. Besides, she really liked seeing Max so coolly in control. When his dictates weren't leveled at her, the power was a real turn-on.

"You don't mean to be disrespectful to Ms. Karas, do you, Randolph? By now I'm sure you know that we weren't having an affair before Friday." Max shot his gaze, neither accusatory nor angry, to Charlie. "And you also know that Ms. Karas thought I was the best man, not the groom, on Friday night. And that Madelyn had left immediately after the rehearsal dinner. And that Leo slipped something into my drink.''

Randolph huffed. This man didn't like being thwarted any more than he liked being wrong. ''Leo told me about your liaison shortly after Madelyn called to announce your supposed elopement. I knew then that she was lying and assumed it was to save face after your rejection. I decided to use the pictures to force you out of the Pier deal, as payback for hurting my daughter. I didn't know until Madelyn called tonight that she'd been the one to cancel the wedding because she didn't love you. But the newspaper's involvement was Leo's doing alone. I wanted this to be a private matter.''

''Well, that didn't happen and neither will my abandoning the development of the Pier.'' Max stood. He'd obviously heard all he came to hear. He glanced at Randolph, who remained seated, then held out his hand to Ariana.

''Randolph, let me give you a piece of advice. Next time you have a concern over your daughter, why don't you actually break down and have a conversation with her? Talk to her instead of trying to just take over and micromanage her life. That's why she left, you know.''

As he let out an exhausted sigh, Randolph's shoulders sagged. ''So I've learned, the hard way.'' He locked gazes with Ariana, but whatever he intended to say to her caught in his throat. He turned back to Max. ''I'll call each of the investors today and assure them of my support of the deal—my support of you, Maxwell.''

He attempted eye contact with Ariana again. "Ms. Karas, I'm not certain there's anything I can do to compensate you for your unfortunate involvement."

Ariana's dark eyebrows arched above wide eyes. "Speaking to me with respect is a very good start, Mr. Burrows. But other than that, no, there's nothing you can do." She stood and extended her hand, but pulled back briefly just as Randolph was about to accept her handshake. "Wait, there is one thing...." She took his proffered hand and held it firmly in hers. "I ran away from my father, from my family, for much the same reasons Maddie ran from you. But I did it when I was a lot younger."

The regret in her voice was a sound Max hadn't heard before. She'd always talked about her emancipation with a tinge of romantic adventure, but comparing her circumstance to Maddie's showed him the sacrifice she'd made in leaving home. He braced a hand on her shoulder.

"Show your daughter some respect when she gets back, Mr. Burrows. She cooked up her engagement to please you. She ran away to please herself. You'd better give her a reason to stay home, or she won't. You'll lose her forever, and that's not good for either of you." She pumped his hand gently, obviously as aware as Max was of the moist glaze that had formed over the man's eyes.

"Come on, Uncle Randy," Charlie said, breaking the somber mood with the endearment, "let's go check on Aunt Barbara."

Without argument, Randolph released Ari's hand

and followed his nephew out. They shut the door behind them, leaving Max and Ari alone.

"Well," Ariana said with a sigh. "That's that. No more photographers. No more lies. What do we do now?"

Max encircled her waist with his arms and tucked her against his chest. "I have an idea, if you're not too exhausted."

She leaned back just far enough to look into his eyes. "Too exhausted for one of your ideas? I can't imagine."

16

JUST BEFORE DAWN, Max wove his way up the road to the top of Twin Peaks in a borrowed pickup with Ariana snuggled beside him. The hills, the second and third tallest vantage points in the city, were nearly deserted in the early-morning hours. A few joggers huffed toward the top. A group of bicyclists congregated toward the bottom, stretching and checking their bikes in preparation for a grueling uphill run. Max had heard about the dazzling panoramic view of the city from here, but he'd never seen it. And with the sunrise, he anticipated the sights would be magnificent. Though not nearly as magnificent as the woman beside him.

He drove until he spied a quiet and secluded spot on the hill, well beyond the paved spaces earmarked for tour buses and tourists.

Daybreak was close at hand, but the skyline still sparkled as they parked. Ariana dug a blanket out of the compartment behind the seat.

"Uncle Stephano used to take Aunt Sonia here all the time," she explained. "It's supposed to be a stunning view."

Ariana pulled her jacket closer and bounded out of the truck before he could tell her the only stunning view he needed could be had by looking at her. She released the latch on the flatbed and climbed aboard, tossed open the metal trunk and then spread a second blanket for them to sit on.

"This is your way to beat the cold?" Max got out of the truck, somewhat disappointed that she planned to rely on thick wool rather than good loving to heat their chilly skin.

She made a show of looking both right and left. They were alone, although that could change at any moment. "I've had my fill of public displays, Max."

He climbed onto the truck bed. "Can't argue that point."

He sat with his back against the cab and held out the other blanket until Ariana snuggled in beside him. She held a bottle of wine and two glasses.

"Your uncle is one prepared guy," he quipped.

Ariana laughed as she dug for the corkscrew and adeptly popped the cork. "Stephano only donated the use of his truck. I brought the wine. After I found Leo, I was planning on surprising you at your house."

He accepted the full glass of something dark and sweet-smelling, but only swirled the liquid while she poured her own glassful and then set the bottle aside.

"You shouldn't have gone after Leo alone, Ari. And I'm not saying that because I want to control you or tell you what to do..."

"I know."

"E-excuse me?"

She grinned at his sputtered response. "I'm obsessive about doing things my own way. I'd like to say it's a hard habit to break but, truth is, it's a reflex I've developed after getting hurt. First by my family not trusting me to run the restaurant. Then by Rick not trusting me to breathe without his direction.''

''Things happen,'' he said, adjusting the blanket so he could slip his arm around her. ''It's human nature to protect yourself any way you can.''

''Even at the expense of love?''

She locked her gaze with his. Max saw the hopeful uncertainty lingering in her eyes and recognized the emotion as exactly what he was feeling himself.

''Love is the first thing we seem to sacrifice,'' he admitted. He most definitely had—in the past, but not anymore. ''Pretty stupid, huh?''

She glanced down into the dark depths of her wineglass. ''I don't know if it's stupid or not.''

She took a sip, then twisted around to abandon her glass on top of the metal trunk they were leaning against. When she turned back, her expression was so stricken, so utterly confused, Max couldn't bear the agony of watching her not know that he loved her, that he was willing to sacrifice everything he owned, now and in the future, to have her love him the way he loved her. With his hand still behind her, he pressed her flush against him and captured her mouth before she could say another word.

Over the past four days, they'd touched a thousand times. Each press of lips, each act of intimacy, had paled compared to this simple kiss. He wanted nothing more than to hold her, feel her connected to him. A part of him. Forever.

She pulled away, her eyes sad. ''I can't do this, Max.''

"Can't do what?"

"Pretend I don't love you!"

His heart swelled. "Who asked you to?"

"No one. You. Me. We were supposed to be together only for this one week. How can we make it work beyond this? I can't give up the restaurant."

"And I'd never ask you to."

"So you want to have a relationship on stolen moments? Breaks from the dinner crowd? How about when you get bogged under with construction at Pier Nine? I'm just organizing the renovation of one restaurant and I can't believe how much time and effort and energy it takes."

"You know, for someone who can instigate some incredible spontaneous excursions, you think too much."

"I think too much?"

Max couldn't believe the words forming in his brain. Since he'd known Ariana Karas, he'd become another person, a better person. The man he had been destined to become before his quest for financial stability overtook his life. He wasn't fooling himself. Accepting these changes wouldn't be any easier for him than they would be for her. But he was willing to make the effort...if she was.

"We'll make it work."

"How?"

"I don't know exactly. And that's the beauty of it. We don't have to know. I didn't know anything about Chinatown until you took me on a tour. You didn't know we were going out on the Bay until I took you to the boat. But we had wonderful adventures without a plan.'' He set his wineglass next to hers, needing both his hands to capture her cheeks, hold her steady while he convinced her they could make this work. ''We'll *both* have to change our ways, Ari, not just you. I love you too much.''

''You do?''

''Didn't you know that? Couldn't you tell? I've never loved anyone before, Ariana. And you know what? I'd go back on food stamps if that's what it took to have you in my life. All these years, I never really understood my parents. How they stayed together when they had nothing.''

''But they didn't have nothing,'' she said.

He nodded, able to agree with all his heart now that this week with her had taught him the truth. ''They had love and passion. Commitment. We could have that to. We can have everything we want.''

''I'm afraid, Max.''

''Of course you are. So am I. It's great, isn't it?''

A glow of new sunlight pinkened the sky just behind Max, adding a phosphorescent glow to the challenge in his eyes. She swallowed, tasting the lingering wine, remembering the feel of his kiss. '''Great' isn't the word I'd choose. I don't like being afraid.''

Max's mouth twisted into a mischievous grin. ''That's because you're afraid of too many things.''

She gasped loudly. ''What? There's the fear of heights and the fear of…'' What? Loving him? No, that didn't really scare her at all. The act was elemental, natural to the woman she'd become over the past few days. Was she afraid of losing herself in Max the way she had with Rick? No, that wasn't it either.

Max loved her, respected her. He'd never allow her to abandon the dreams and ambitions and quirks that made her who she was.

As the dawn brightened, the impatience in his gaze grew more and more obvious. She tugged her bottom lip with her teeth. She feared losing him, but one glance into those dark green eyes and she knew that her fear was completely unfounded.

"You won't leave me, will you?"

He only shook his head. That's all she needed. The rest she knew with her own heart.

"Okay, then I'm just afraid of heights."

Max's mouth twitched, then he stood quickly, drawing her up into his arms with a bounce. "Let's see if we can't take care of that one, too."

"What?"

Before she could react, he swung her up on top of the cab of the truck. Parked on the precipice as they were, she glanced down and felt as if she was about to tumble onto the slowly waking city.

"Ack! Max!"

He let go of her long enough to climb up beside her. Their combined weight dented the top with a metallic pop.

"Oh, God!" she gasped. The man was insane! Wonderful, handsome, giving beyond belief, but certifiably crazy.

And so was she. Crazy in love.

"Don't worry about the truck," he assured her, grabbing her by the waist when her legs failed to move. "I'll buy Stephano a new one."

"I'm not worried about the truck. Yes, I am. Is the emergency brake on? Max! We're going to fall."

He moved her in front of him and wrapped his arms around her waist. Curving his body around her, he buried his face in her hair, inhaled, then nuzzled her neck. "Too late. I've fallen for you, Ariana Karas, and there is nothing you can do about it."

She closed her eyes, focusing all her attention, all her rioting nerves, on the feel of him holding her, steadying her, erasing the overwhelming dizziness caused by the vertigo, until all that was left was her light-headed reaction to being in love.

"If that's the only falling you plan for us to do today, then I'll survive."

His chuckle renewed her sense of impending danger. "I want you to more than survive, sweetheart. Open your eyes."

"They're open," she lied.

He cleared his throat. "Ariana, do you remember the last time you wouldn't open your eyes when I told you to?"

"When we made love on the balcony," she admitted, hardly needing to think to recall the sensual means he'd used then to convince her. "Wait a minute! I thought you didn't remember that night?"

Her eyes flashed open in protest, just in time to catch the wiggle in his eyebrows. "Little bits and pieces have been coming back, mostly in dreams. All of them so decadent I thought they might have just been naughty fantasies."

She huffed back into the safety net of his arms. "You should have told me."

"We have a few days left of our wild week. I thought I'd show you."

He pulled her fully against him, his hard arousal pressed to her back. One arm held her steady, wrapped protectively across her midsection while his other hand wandered down her thigh, then up, skirting beneath her blazer over her ribs.

"I thought we were done making love out in the open, Max."

"Who's making love?" he asked innocently. "I'm not making love. I'm just touching you, holding you, showing you the city in the dawn of a new day."

Though the sensations of his touch made her vision hazy, she picked out a few famous sites they'd yet to visit. The top of the pyramid-like Transamerica Building. The round, nozzle shape of Coit Tower. The vast green expanse of Golden Gate Park. But with Max's hands wandering, brushing over her breast, skimming the top of her waistband, she couldn't think of any sight more attractive than that California king at his house.

She twisted around until she faced him, rocking unsteadily despite his tightly coiled embrace. Her fear of heights was obviously going to take a little longer to overcome than her fear of falling in love. And she'd never felt freer in her entire life.

"We've got the rest of our lives to see the city, Ari. I just want to see you. Naked. In my bed, your bed, anywhere."

"Anywhere?"

He laughed. "Don't tempt me. I'd make love to

you right here if I had my way. Maybe I am an exhibitionist at heart.''

''And that's just one thing I love about you,'' she said with a smile.

He kissed her deep and long, until she nearly forgot they were standing on the cab of a truck parked at the top of the hill. With the wind and the warming sun, she imagined they were floating on a cloud.

''What I really want is for you to marry me.'' He whispered the proposal in her ear, then leaned back just enough to gauge her reaction.

Only she didn't have a reaction. She didn't know what to do or what to say. She'd never dreamed... never guessed. ''Max, that's a big leap. Are you sure?''

''I wouldn't have asked if I wasn't sure. Take the leap with me, Ariana. I promise we'll make it.''

Ariana lifted herself completely into his arms, then jumped up and wrapped her legs around him while shouting like someone who'd just won the lottery. She didn't care who heard her. She didn't care who saw. She was going to marry the man she loved with all her heart and soul. And knew their union would last for a lifetime.

Because she knew firsthand that Max was a man of his word.

HARLEQUIN® *Blaze*™

presents...

Four erotic interludes that could occur
only during...

Sexy
CITY NIGHTS

EXPOSED! by *Julie Elizabeth Leto*
Blaze #4—August 2001
Looking for love in sizzling San Francisco...

BODY HEAT by *Carly Phillips*
Blaze #8—September 2001
Risking it all in decadent New York...

HEAT WAVES by *Janelle Denison*
Blaze #12—October 2001
Finding the ultimate fantasy in fiery Chicago...

L.A. CONFIDENTIAL by *Julie Kenner*
Blaze #16—November 2001
Living the dream in seductive Los Angeles...

SEXY CITY NIGHTS—
Where the heat escalates *after* dark!

And don't miss out on reading about naughty New Orleans
in ONE WICKED WEEKEND, a weekly online serial
by Julie Elizabeth Leto, available now at www.eHarlequin.com!

Visit us at www.tryblaze.com   HBSCN

Montana Matchmakers

Bestselling author

Kristine Rolofson

invites you to Bliss, Montana,
and the annual matchmaking
contest! Look for this sexy,
fun new trilogy:

#842 *A Wife for Owen Chase*
(August 2001)

#850 *A Bride for Calder Brown*
(October 2001)

#858 *A Man for Maggie Moore*
(December 2001)

MONTANA MATCHMAKERS
*Find the perfect match
in Big Sky Country!*

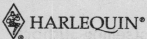

Get *caught* up with the hot NEW single title from

LORI FOSTER

CAUGHT IN THE ACT

COINCIDENCE? Not.

Mick Dawson, undercover cop. He's got his hands full with a pushy broad who claims she's just in the wrong place at the wrong time. Except all the perps seem to know everything there is to know about her. Who're you going to believe? Only one way to find out. Get *really* close.

Lela DeBraye (aka Delta Piper), mystery writer. She's as confused as he is, but mostly because he's got the sweetest smile, when he smiles. Still, he's sticking with her twenty-four/seven—is this love or duty? Is he her protector or her captor?

Look for *CAUGHT IN THE ACT* in September 2001.

LOOK FOR OUR EXCITING

HARLEQUIN® Blaze™

RED-HOT READS

NEXT MONTH!

Including:

THIRTY NIGHTS by JoAnn Ross
THE PLEASURE PRINCIPLE by Kimberly Raye
UNINHIBITED by Candace Schuler
BODY HEAT by Carly Phillips

HARLEQUIN®
Makes any time special®

Visit us at www.tryblaze.com

HBUSCOUPON2

LOOK FOR OUR EXCITING

HARLEQUIN® *Blaze*™

RED-HOT READS

NEXT MONTH!

Including:

THIRTY NIGHTS by JoAnn Ross

THE PLEASURE PRINCIPLE by Kimberly Raye

UNINHIBITED by Candace Schuler

BODY HEAT by Carly Phillips

HARLEQUIN®
Makes any time special ®

Visit us at www.tryblaze.com

HBCANCOUPON2

Brimming with passion and sensuality,
this collection offers two full-length
Harlequin Temptation novels.

Full Bloom

by *New York Times* bestselling author

JAYNE
—— ANN ——
KRENTZ

Emily Ravenscroft has had enough! It's time she took her life back,
out of the hands of her domineering family and Jacob Stone, the
troubleshooter they've always employed to get her out of hot water.
The new Emily—vibrant and willful—doesn't need Jacob to rescue
her. She needs him to love her, against all odds.

And

Compromising Positions

a brand-new story from bestselling author

VICKY LEWIS
THOMPSON

Look for it on sale September 2001.